THE SCAPEG0AT

HOW A NETWORK, A CONFERENCE RIVAL, AND A
COMMISSIONER CRUCIFIED A COACH TO
ACCOMPLISH THEIR OWN SELFISH AGENDAS

LANE ALPERT

A BLOOD IN THE WATER NOVEL

The Scapegoat
Copyright © 2017 by Lane Alpert and Blood in the Water

Requests for information should be emailed to:
bloodinthewater9@gmail.com

ISBN: 1979830266
ISBN-13: 978-1979830263

Dear Reader –

The Scapegoat is based on true events. If you are a college football fan, the events are eerily similar to the internet articles you read and saw on television. The story is fiction. All the characters' personalities and their conversations are created for the novel to tell a compelling story. It should not be considered an "investigative report" since all the information used to construct the novel was public information. Truth is stranger than fiction..........maybe.

Regardless, may you find a cause worthy of a fight.

Remember the Alamo!!

Lane Alpert

In honor -

Davy Crockett – *Who fought for a cause that was not his "fight".*

My friend, **Matt Price** *(The Price Factor) – who was a modern day Davy Crockett.*

To the men who played 2016 football in Waco. *You were deserted by an administration. You were coached by a distracted staff. You were attacked by the national media, the conference and your opponents. You were left on your own. You were, however, supported by the fans and the one who recruited you. Persevere!*

ACKNOWLEDGMENTS

Thanks to my beautiful wife who has endured this year and half long project. Thanks to my family, who patiently listened and heard the story repeated during that time. I am grateful for my good friends and sounding boards – Brooks Allen, Brig Jones and Brian Farr. The book could not have happened without the incredible editing support of Pigeon O'Brien, Jeff Nagle, Tom Osterholt Jr and Jeff Duke. Special thanks for their contribution to the project – Steve Hughes, Mike Weinberg, Bret Mason, and Jennifer Stolzer.

The search for a **scapegoat** is the easiest of all hunting expeditions." — **Dwight** D. **Eisenhower**

Prologue
(Jerusalem 750 BC)

The Day of Atonement was rapidly approaching and soon the city would be packed and crowded. The high priest summoned two other priests and the ready man, all sons of Aaron, to prepare the offering. The high priest would perform the ceremony, but the others were needed for preparation. One priest was assigned the task of finding and bringing to the temple courts the sacrificed bull, which was to be offered for his own sin to make atonement for himself and his household.

The second priest was responsible for finding two male goats to offer as a sin offering for the people. He would cast lots to determine which goat was to be burnt and which was for *gezarah*. Gezarah comes from the Hebrew word *gazar* which means to cut off, or exclude. The ready man would be assigned the task of taking the goat away from the city to the land of gezarah.

For years they had carried out their assignments as the Lord had instructed. Each priest was always willing to help the high priest. The sins of the people were many. So each priest took his assignment seriously in order to please the Lord.

On the Day of Atonement, the two goats were brought before the high priest. The lots were cast. The first goat was slaughtered. The high priest took the blood as instructed and went behind the curtain to the Most Holy place and sprinkled the blood on the Mercy Seat. The blood represented the uncleanliness and the rebellion of Israel.

When this was complete, the second goat, the live one, was brought to the high priest. He placed both hands over the goat's head and confessed over it all the peoples' wicked sins. When he was finished, the goat was given to the ready man.

The ready man took the goat with all the sins to a solitary place, the wilderness. Sometime a few hours later, the ready man released the goat into the desert. The animal was termed the Scapegoat; it was "cut off," never to return to the city again.

The Scapegoat

Cast of Characters

The Network Alliance

The Network: The largest sports broadcasting network. Media outlets are cable television, magazine, radio and the Internet. It has an exclusive TV channel devoted solely to the State University.

The Network Executive: The decision maker for the Network's programming and broadcasting. He is responsible for signing the contracts with the Power 5 conferences and for buying university networks.

The Department Head: The person who runs the investigative department for The Network. His unit is part of programming and his boss is the Network Executive.

The Reporter: A journalist for the Network's investigative unit. She reports directly to the Department Head and is often a key note speaker at investigative reporting trade events.

The Victim: A student who pressed charges against a Baptist University football player for sexual assault. She filed a lawsuit against the school and its head coach. The Network used her in several of its broadcasts.

The Advocate: A spokesperson for rape and sexual assault survivors. She was and is hired to speak at schools all over the country to share her personal story of sexual assault. She is an outspoken antagonist against the Baptist University and its football team. The Network invites her to comment on some of its broadcasts.

The Scapegoat

The Conference Rival (State University) Alliance

The State University: Largest state school in Texas.

The State University Network: Broadcasting company for the University. It was sold to the Network.

The Chancellor: Head of the State University and a member of the executive committee of the conference. He is a friend to the Commissioner of the conference.

The Booster: Alumnus and big money donor as well as part owner of the State University Network. He is friends with the Network Executive and the Commissioner.

Blogger/Radio Host: Renowned local personality and broadcaster who primarily covers the State University. He is friends with Network's Reporter and Department Head.

Multinational news agency: A worldwide news reporting source that releases news articles in local markets. The local representative covers the State University.

Largest sport's magazine: Nation's largest and oldest sports publication. Magazine is produced bi-weekly. The local writer covers the State University.

Social media wiz: Die-hard fan of the State University. He is an expert at finding articles and statements and posting them on Twitter and other social media. .

The Writer: A free- lance journalist and author. She teaches journalism classes at the State University.

Software Developer: Owner of a technology company in Capitol City, Texas. He is friends with the Writer. Avid fan.

The Commissioner Alliance

The Commissioner: He is the salaried head of the conference and is responsible for representing the conference for contractual agreements. He presides over meetings and conference forums and panels and is friends with the Network Executive.

The Executive Committee of the Conference: Comprised of the three presidents at the State University, the Other State University and the Great Plains University.

The Conference Panel on Sexual Assault: Established by the Commissioner. The Reporter and the Advocate are members along with others.

Network Executive
(Spring 2012, New England)

"Shit! Shit! Shit!" The Network Executive shouted as he banged his desk with his hands. It was a bad deal. He knew it was a bad deal. His gut told him it was a bad deal but his head and the brainiac Ivy League kid in market research convinced him otherwise.

Of course there is no such thing as bad projections, he said to himself. It wasn't the fifteen million dollar a year loss that was eating him. The network company was worth hundreds of millions. The corporate company that owned the network was worth billions. No one would ever notice the loss hidden amongst all the gains. But it was his decision, and he hated making bad decisions. He never used the word "mistakes." Mistakes could be corrected, bad decisions could not.

He was a fast tracker. He was a college athlete, not an Ivy Leaguer or a Division I player. He graduated from a highly academic parochial school and he had the nose and the drive to make successful business deals. None of his work associates were surprised when he was awarded the title, Director of Programming for the Network.

His golden ticket was college sports. Early in his career he knew how popular college basketball and college football would become. It wasn't just the sellout games, the addition of bowl games and later college playoffs, or the increase in ticket prices. It was the enthusiasm of the fans that he monitored.

Tailgating would start a couple days before the game started. Fifty year old men would face-paint. Vegas gambling for college football was about to surpass NFL betting. It was the internet and the rise of message boards, where fans wanted to talk about their college teams. They could freely criticize and cut down their opponents. Because they could use slick monikers like, "Lumberjack Loyal "and "StateUsucks", they could passionately, under the guise of anonymity, say anything they wanted. This passion for college sports translated into higher profits for the Network.

He had made it his goal to lock up the broadcasting rights for all the teams that were members of the Power 5 conferences. He was willing to pay twenty to twenty-five million dollars a year for those broadcasting rights. They were the best teams with the largest audiences, which translated into the greatest revenue dollars. While it *sounded* ridiculous to have a conference name not match the same number of teams in each conference, no one cared! The fans loved the association of being in a Power 5 conference.

The broadcasting rights would keep out the competition. The Network would choose the best games to broadcast and they would farm out the less popular games to other stations. The State University creating its own network presented new challenges. He knew he would have to pay extra each year to the State University to buy its network. While he believed in long term contracts, he was now questioning himself on his decision.

Who signs a twenty year contract? Who signs a deal where all the startup costs are absorbed in the contract price? Who signs a contract that still gives the selling entity rights to have any employee fired who does not reflect the interests of the State University, the primary benefactor? Who signs a contract that once the sales price break-even occurs, the selling entity still gets seventy percent of the ongoing profit?

There was no one else to blame. Programming contracts were his decisions. The Network Executive was responsible for the signing.

The deal ultimately caused two schools to leave the conference. Their departure ended the North and South divisions and the championship game. The Network Executive did not necessarily trust the Chancellor or the Booster, who had a vested interest in the contract, but they were all correct: Football is king in Texas.

Texas produces the best players nationwide. The majority of colleges recruit down there. So many Texas high school seniors could play at the next level as true college freshman, bypassing the red shirt process. It was truly remarkable what the State University had accomplished by helping create its own broadcasting network. Its ability to televise high school games would give them a recruiting advantage. It was pure genius. The Network Executive loved pure genius.

His gut told him the sub-.500 season in the recent past may not have been a fluke. The Booster and the Chancellor of the state school assured him it was exactly a fluke. They knew Texas. They loved their state and their state university.

The Network Executive signed the contract.

The Commissioner
(Spring 2012, BIG D, Texas)

The plan was for this job to be the last one until retirement. His children were grown. They were a non-factor in his decision. His wife had fallen in love with the Pacific Ocean, the allure of the wine country, the weather, and the prestige of his position as Athletic Director for an elite west coast private university.

The Commissioner's wife was not thrilled about a move to Texas, where the conference headquarters were located. The big hair and the big personalities she found audacious. The Commissioner assured her that with an annual salary of two and a half million dollars, they would be able to afford two homes. She would have ample time to visit their children and future grandchildren. It was Big D, Texas where they would live, he reminded her. And Big D was cosmopolitan. She could make it work. The "y'alls" would not bother her. Cowboy boots were making a fashion comeback. Two close airports would make traveling easy. Her husband argumentatively had a plethora of reasons for why the move was a good idea. She reluctantly agreed to the move and the acceptance of her husband's new position.

He was selected to be the commissioner of the conference because of his experience, connections and unflappable personality. He was hired to negotiate the conference's new broadcasting contract that was coming up for renewal. His goal was to negotiate a contract that was in par with the other Power 5 conferences. He knew the Network was hungry to get the last conference signed to a long term deal.

The Commissioner said to himself, "Just don't screw anything up and all will be good. Really good."

Anything he did would be an improvement from his predecessor. The previous commissioner watched the conference fall apart, almost to the point of being dissolved. Four state powerhouses had left the conference for more lucrative revenue earnings opportunities with other conferences. This exodus screwed up scheduling; it abruptly put an end to a crowning championship game.

While the remaining school presidents wanted to blame the previous commissioner for not keeping the conference together, the reality is that two schools - two large state schools - had the power and controlled the conference. They knew the conference could not exist without them. But the four exiting schools had had enough. When it was announced that one of the conference schools was going to start its own broadcasting network, that included televising high school football games, the four leaving schools inked their deals elsewhere. They would be unable to competitively recruit in Texas.

The good news for the conference was that they had two schools eagerly ready and willing to join a Power 5 Conference. One of the schools was a small private university (Private University) already located in the geographical footprint of that conference. The other school (Coal Miner State University) was far east, but it had a strong athletic history. The higher level of athletic competition exceeded the cost and the logic of its far distance from the other schools in the conference.

The Commissioner was needed to sign the contract. Make the conference happy. Make the Network happy. It was simple. Finding two more schools to join the conference would ultimately be handled by the Network. The candidates would line up. He had seen the contracts from the other conferences. While the revenue to the schools was obscene, the penalties for leaving a conference were financially severe: No Power 5 School could jump to another conference without economically hurting itself. Besides, the revenue payouts were so similar, what would be the point? Any new additions to his new conference would be from smaller Division I schools that could prove themselves athletically worthy. But once again, it was not his problem.

He had grown reading Mad magazine. He chuckled at the mental image of his face being morphed with that of Alfred E. Neuman saying "What, me worry?"

He sat at his new desk, in his new office thinking about his future. This would be his last job before retirement. If he stayed five years in the position, he could retire a wealthy man. But he saw himself in this role even longer. The network contract he would negotiate would be a long term deal. He would retire before the network contract expired. He wrote his 10 year goals on the back of a Conference envelope:

1) Negotiate network deal.
2) Keep the two big conference state schools happy.
3) If in doubt, see #2.

He smiled to himself as he read them again. He crunched the envelope into a ball and threw it into the trash can under his desk.

He was on his way to an appointment, but as he passed his newly assigned Texas administrative assistant, he tapped on her desk and said, "What, me worry?"

The Chancellor
(Spring 2012, Capitol City, Texas)

He was not allowed to smoke in the buildings, nor anywhere on campus but that did not stop him from chewing on his cigar. He loved the taste, but mostly he had the cigar as a nervous habit to calm himself down. He had also made a promise to his wife, a long ago, that he'd give up Copenhagen. Dipping was a habit that every West Texas young man develops to take off the edge and relax. Besides, as a renowned doctor, smoking would appear hypocritical. Cigar chewing was acceptable.

Something was bothering him, but he could not put his finger on the problem. It was a sixth sense. He had an ominous feeling that something bad was going to happen. His gut kept going back to the State University's football team. His medical training reminded him to just deal with the facts.

Fact: He had one of the best coaches in all of college football. He was legendary (viewed nationally as one of the best).

Fact: Last ten years: One National Championship, One runner-up, and three other Top ten finishes.

Fact: The State University won its most recent bowl game.

Fact: The Network had bought out its university network, which was dropping an additional fifteen million dollars to the school's bottom line. Fifteen million dollars was more than any other school in the conference was receiving.

Fact: Both he and the Athletic Director (AD) had access to the executives at the Network and could influence and control the programming and the spin on particular stories.

Fact: The Booster was making a lot of money. The Booster was giving a lot of money,

The negatives?

Fact: Season before last, the State University had its only losing season since the legendary coach had taken over.

Fact: The football team lost more games in the last two seasons than the previous nine combined.

Fact: It had lost some of the best high school recruits to the irrelevant Baptist University up the road over the last couple years.

Fact: The irrelevant Baptist school had put together two winning seasons in a row. It was the first time in fifteen years the Baptist football team had been to a bowl game.

"WTF," the Chancellor thought. "Why?"

Baptist had a terrible stadium. Its alumni were small and subdued compared to the other schools in Texas. Games never sold out, and the fan attendance was low when the team played on the road.

"I don't get it. It makes no sense," his brain kept at it.

His phone rang. He looked down. It was the Booster. He let the call go to voicemail, along with the twenty-seven other calls that morning.

"Unbelievable!," He watched the phone message light blink unattended. "The Booster truly thinks we should be in the running for a national championship every year- just because we are the State University!" It seemed idiotic.

Almost immediately, the phone rang again. It was an internal call from his "inside" person in the Athletic Department. This call he had to take. There was a big divide between the athletic department and the administration. It was this way at every school. He was damn sure the rich Texas boosters-and now this mandated Title IX office with a mandated coordinator-was preparing to make the division between the two even worse.

"Hello?" the Chancellor said.

The voice on the other end said quietly. "He's here again." The Chancellor didn't speak.

"The same person got in the same car again," the caller said.

"Follow him and report back where he stopped," said the Chancellor. "I don't like it. Are you sure Legendary Coach does not know?"

"There's no way," the voice on the other end replied. "They're tight. Or they *were* tight. Do you want me to tell him?

"No, not yet," the Chancellor said. "That's a can of worms that I'm not ready to open at the moment. Keep me posted. I appreciate the eyes and ears."

He hung up the phone.

The Chancellor looked off in deep thought. Although their programming was different, the movie cable network was a competitor of The Network. Why would the Sports Host from the largest movie cable network be meeting with the Director of Football Operations? And why does the Legendary Coach not know about it?

The Chancellor's policy was, "If I know about it, the hammer is coming down." So he made sure everyone knew *he* did not want to know about it.

He wasn't sure if he had swallowed a piece of his cigar, or if his worst case scenario thoughts were getting the best of him. He had a premonition that something bad was about to happen. He just had a sickening feeling in his stomach. Instinctively, he reached for a can of

Copenhagen in his back pocket. Of course, nothing was there.

The Coach
(Spring 2012, Central Texas)

You either loved him or you hated him, there was no in between. He was a player's coach. Players loved him. When his team lost The Coach always blamed himself. When his team won, the victory was attributed to the players for their performance. Even though he didn't attend Baptist University, Baptist Nation adopted him as its own son. They loved him. The other conference schools hated him. The other conferences' coaches hated him. The alumni and fans from the other conference schools – hated him. Except for the true football experts and those from the South, the media hated him.

He loved Texas. He loved football. You only had to be around him for thirty seconds to find that out. Once he was asked about his favorite restaurant. He knew there would be one right answer and a thousand wrong ones. So he replied, "Anything with the name Texas in it, I know it's going to be good."

He played the game. He knew the game. In a ball cap and long sleeved athletic wear, he would march along the sidelines. Just his presence commanded respect. He was born to coach football. In the rare times where he was seen in a suit or sports coat, he looked uncomfortable and was almost unrecognizable. Football was his life.

There is a reason football was his life: it gave him purpose and a way out when he faced his darkest time. His parents died in an accident on their way to watch one of his games when he was in college. He never got to say goodbye. Instead, he had to heal from a physical injury that plagued his season. He had to heal from the huge trauma of the loss of his parents. He had nowhere to turn. Football became his focus. Football gave him the motivation to press forward. Football gave him a meaningful distraction to numb the pain.

It took him years to be able to talk about the pain, and the loss. He never wanted the attention. He never wanted to use it as a crutch, making excuses why bad things in his life happened. It took years to gain the perspective that bad things happen to people, even him. Now he would freely talk about it to encourage his players so that when they face tough personal issues, they too can use football as a means to move their lives forward. But for a long time, the pain was a secret he kept.

When he took the job at the Baptist University, his family thought he was crazy. It was a job nobody wanted. The school had twelve previous seasons without a winning record; fifteen seasons without a Bowl win. They were the "homecoming game" for other teams. They were the doormat of the conference.

To turn the program around seemed like an impossible task.

The Coach took the job because he liked challenges. He had a successful history turning around football programs. He'd revived other high school and college football teams with longer histories of losing. He hated to lose. He knew that to turn around the Baptist University football program, he'd need successful recruiting. That was going to be the key element. And to ensure successful recruiting, the school would need new facilities, especially a new stadium.

He had a great ability to recruit. He recruited a special kind of player. His criteria were that each player had to either be fast or physically big in size. They had to have an "edge," or a built in desire to be better; race didn't matter to him. It did not matter if a player had two eager parents or were raised by a single, overburdened mother. It did not matter if his recruits were rich or poor. It did not matter if they were straight laced, follow-the-rules types or if they had already fathered a child.

He would make them stronger. He would make them tougher. He could make them love the game. His love for the game and his love for the players created an insatiable comradery. He'd work out with them in the weight room. Practices consisted of playing loud music and running all drills at a hundred percent. He knew you had to make practices fun. He would often let the players design their own plays.

The bond he developed with his players was so tight that he often gave them nicknames. Once a player had a nickname, it remained with him for his whole career at Baptist University. Giving a nickname was a tough guy's way of showing fondness and care.

His first two seasons were rough, losing seasons. The recruits were young but they were getting experience. He had strong relationships with the high school football coaches, which he leveraged for recruiting. The high school coaches knew about his character and work ethic, so it was easy for them to recommend honestly to their players that they should consider playing for Baptist University.

He was able to land a couple strong, highly ranked football recruits. This allowed him to build and surround other players. But Coach knew that the longer he coached at the Baptist University his connections would dry up. They would retire or follow their own career ambitions and move out of high school into college, or the pros. Relationships were not enough. So the upgrade in the campus facilities would need to be a priority.

Early after he was hired by Baptist University, he got to be friends with some of the more influential Regents on the Baptist University Board. He was able to share his vision for a new stadium and for practice facilities adjacent to the campus. While it was only a vision, he had no idea that during the spring of 2012 how much time and effort he would have to spend to make the vision a reality.

He was trying to run spring practice and get ready for the spring game - an event used to generate excitement for the upcoming fall season. His nights were filled with meeting architects. He was constantly meeting with the administration for updates. He started keeping count in his head how many times he was asked, "How's it going?" and then lost count. But the biggest use of his time came from the Regents and the development office that needed the Coach to be present at the fundraisers or for dinners where he had to play nice with the Regents' influential friends. He showed up for their dinners, answered their questions, and kept them updated when they asked, "How's it going?" He rarely saw his wife and his family.

A couple days after the spring game, the Coach was sitting in his office late one morning. He had just finished watching game film and was making notes when his cell phone vibrated in his pants pocket. He ignored it. He would return calls in the afternoon, a habit he developed as he followed a strict team schedule of practice, work-outs, coaching meetings and film study. Game preparation was something he worked on in the evening. Then, he would make calls and return communication.

The phone vibrated again and again. The first one signaled another call, and then another for a text, and another text. He pulled out phone.

The call was from the Baptist University Judicial Affairs office. It meant one of his players was in trouble. The text confirmed it, when he read "CALL ASAP. WE NEED TO DISCUSS AN INCIDENT INVOLVING ONE OF YOUR PLAYERS."

While he was reading the text, he received another text. This one was from one of the assistant coaches. "WE HAVE AN ISSUE WITH OUR DEFENSIVE PLAYER. I JUST HEARD FROM JUDICIAL AFFAIRS."

The Coach texted back, "Go talk with the player, and call me back."

Coach knew it had to be serious if Judicial Affairs was involved. The texts didn't mention if charges were pressed or if the player had been arrested. While he wanted to pick up the phone and dial someone who could give him more details, he knew he had to wait. He would know more information when his assistant coach checked back. If charges were pressed, the player would be suspended. Depending on severity of the incident, the suspension could be indefinite.

When he first started college coaching as a position coach, it was the position coach's responsibility to deal with the player and deal with the administration when certain off-the-field issues arose. Underage drinking and possession of marijuana were considered minor infractions. Head coaches were not to be involved or included; those were the responsibilities of the assistant coaches. Head coaches were to enforce discipline when a violation of team rules occurred, which would include sitting out a game, or community service. Almost every university in America turned a blind eye to underage drinking, so that was not a concern. Weed? No one cares any more. Four states have legalized it. "Repeat offenses" can't be ignored, however, because a player can only have so many "second chances," and they usually signaled other problems. It always made the coach sad to kick a player off his team for smoking marijuana after so many chances and warnings. He didn't get it. Why would they risk the opportunity to play college football on something so small?

Every major football program is built on an important premise: the head coach is the last to know. This became the unwritten rule ever since a head coach at THE University, located in Ohio, was let go. Even though he didn't know his players traded football gear for tattoos, once the NCAA found email citing a raid at the tattoo parlor, it was determined the coach had failed to respond once he was made aware of the issue. "Better late than never" became the NCAA mode of operation.

Right or wrong, across the country, assaults fell into two different categories: physical and sexual. Physical assaults that involved pushing down or restraining a girlfriend or a woman usually involved some suspension for a player to miss a game or two. Hitting a woman was never tolerated and involved a longer suspension. Some of the elite college football programs were able to hide the assaults and suspend for a year. Other programs would expel the athlete from the school.

The Coach always took the position of encouraging the female victim to press charges. Once charges were pressed the coach could enact the only discipline he was empowered to impose: the player was kicked off the team or suspended from the team. Only the university had the power to expel a student. Pressing charges had to be done because filing a report with school authorities was never enough. Too many accusers never pressed charges. Almost eighty percent of the time, alcohol and drugs were involved in the situation. Victims were too embarrassed to press charges because they were not a hundred percent sure that a sexual assault had actually occurred. This often led to waves of "She said – He Said" that could ruin young lives.

Since football was officially over, it took the Assistant Coach longer than usual to track down the Defensive Player. Late into the afternoon, Coach got a text from the assistant coach. It read, "I tracked down the player. We talked. The player does not even know the girl. Does not know what I'm talking about."

In the past, this would have allowed the Coach to breathe a sigh of relief. Not this time. He'd learned, even with the minor offenses that the first response the players make is to lie. He had heard and read too many stories where the players' first words were, "It was consensual" or, "it was just fun" or "it was just play time, nothing really happened."

He'd wait to call Judicial Affairs tomorrow; he was already late to a dinner with Alumni donors who were ready to pull out the checkbooks for a new stadium. "How's it going?" they were going to ask. He got his smile ready.

The next morning, Coach called Judicial Affairs. He hated making the call. At every place he ever coached there was already an innate division between the athletic department and the administration. The athletic departments made a lot of money for their schools, but administrations didn't like coaches' salaries, which usually topped the administrators, who were annoyed by the perks the student athletes received on top of their scholarships. The Baptist University was no different.

Coach prided his wins on game preparation, studying film, and knowing as much as he could about his opponents' tendencies. The problem with Judicial Affairs was that the information only flowed one way. He was never able to gauge exactly their intent. He felt unprepared. Since the university police department reported directly to Judicial Affairs, he always felt that every question asked of him was a loaded question where Judicial Affairs already knew the answer, and sometimes he was "on trial."

Only twenty percent of the student body lived on campus. Any parties or obnoxious behavior or disturbances were handled by the local municipal police. Local police were not necessarily fans of the Baptist University. Maybe only a few were alumni or attended class at the university. Almost none were parents. The city was primarily a blue collar town and did not have an appetite for upper middle class students coming into their town with pretentious attitudes and fancy ways. So it was not surprising the locals didn't like the University acquiring more real estate. They surely did not like seeing admissions of incoming students increase, especially while their own kids went off to state universities, or to work.

Local police were the ones called whenever an incident occurred off campus. They were the ones who wrote up a police report. Depending on the criminal activity, municipal police were called to investigate. It was their case and their investigation. The local police were under no obligation to share or tell the university police of any wrongdoings by any of its students while situations were investigated and charges formed. The captain of the university police however urged the local police to keep them informed of any issues involving fraternities first and student athletes second, just to keep everyone in the loop.

The Coach punched up the Director of Judicial Affairs on the phone. When he was through, he said, "Sorry for the delay getting back to you. We just finished wrapping up spring ball and I've been buried with the new stadium. What can I do for you?"

The Director of Judicial Affairs abruptly stated, "Are you aware of the situation with your Defensive Player?"

Coach replied, "Only that you talked to my assistant coach. I've been informed that he talked with the player in question, and the Defensive Player does not even know the girl or anything about the incident."

The other end was silent.

"What other information do you need from us?" Coach asked.

"Figures," the director thought to herself. She waited to respond. Such a good ole Texan boy, she thought. She could never tell if his straightforward candor was due to naivety, or if he mastered the art of bluffing. Was he playing her for a fool?

"Are you aware that there are others?" she asked, tersely.

"Other players involved?" Coach asked.

He was not making this easy on the Director. This was rapidly developing and she'd found out earlier in week that there might be other victims. Parents of another woman victim had scheduled an appointment with her. However, a member of the sexual prevention advisory board, a SANE nurse from the local hospital that administers rape kits, had called her recognizing an alleged perpetrator's name.

"No. Victims. There may be other women," she told him. A part of her wondered if he even cared.

"Charges pressed?" the Coach questioned.

"Not yet," the director allowed. "But it looks like the parents are in town so I'm expecting a formal student complaint to be filed on that level. We'll be meeting with your player soon. Goodbye," she said, and hung up before waiting for the Coach's reply.

The coach immediately texted the assistant coach, "GO TALK TO HIM AGAIN. TEXT ME BACK."

Two hours later the reply came back. "He admitted he lied to us. When she said stop, he stopped." Since the coach was left out in the dark, he was more confused. He asked himself, what's going on? Multiple girls? Does this player even know which girl said what?

Coach wasn't a drinker, but he was a thinker. He pocketed his phone, walked outside, got in his truck and drove. As he drove, thoughts came. He was sad. He had daughters of his own. He was sad for the defensive football player because he knew he was a father of two young sons. He was sad because this player was taking football seriously and was set back by a knee injury at the end of last season. He was sad because this same player had been caught plagiarizing semesters ago. Coach had written a special letter to the president of the Baptist University to show consideration, to give him a second chance, to keep him in school. He believed football was the Defensive Player's way to provide for his family and improve his life.

Pounding the steering wheel, and laying on the horn, Coach yelled, "What have you done?!" Only a couple of cattle nosing grass turned their heads at the noisy truck speeding down the country road.

One and a half weeks later, when a warrant from a municipal judge was issued, the assistant coach texted "Police coming. Oral swabs for DNA."

The Coach text back, "Not good."

That Friday, the Coach kicked the player off the team. Early the following week, the player was arrested for sexual assault. Three weeks passed; during that time the university had final exams. The player was expelled from Baptist University.

The Commissioner
(Winter 2012, Big D, Texas)

Sitting at his desk, looking out the window, the Commissioner was reflecting. It had been a long time since he enjoyed the winters where snow drifted down and covered everything. He doubted he would ever see a Texas winter with snow.

It had been a successful year. The contract he negotiated was better than expected. The conference presidents were pleased they were receiving revenues that were even higher than some of the other conferences. All was good.

He wished he'd kept the old envelope where he had written his goals. Goal #1 had been accomplished. The football season could not have ended better. One of the large state schools was co-champion of the conference, the other state school finished second.

Goal #2- Keep the two large state schools happy. Done.

He tried to stay away from conference rumors. There was no point in getting involved or asking if they were true. He did find it amusing; that one of the large state schools was going to replace its legendary coach at the end of the 2013 season. It was rumored that the front runner was the head coach of Baptist University.

It made sense to him. The Baptist University coach had no real ties to the university. The Commissioner was unsure if the coach was even Baptist. The Coach's son even played football elsewhere, at the State University. He was a recruiting powerhouse and the State University was probably going to throw a large contract his way. With the bump in revenue sharing from the Network and the extra fifteen million dollars that the school received due to the sale of its university network, more power to them for offering a pile of money. He just smiled.

Goal #2 – Keep the two large state schools happy.

He was in such a good mood; a stop at the Galleria was in order to buy his wife some nice Christmas presents.

The Chancellor
(Mid-Fall 2013, Capitol City, Texas)

A month ago, he thought the football program had dodged a bullet. His inside person in the Athletic Department reported that the Sports Host from the movie cable network never returned. Every week, his inside person would report which outside media was showing up with cameras. Of course, they knew their own network reporters. They maintained tight leashes around the national guys who consisted of the largest sports magazine publication, the multinational news agency, the internet agency that covered the school and the coveted bulldog "hard hitting" internet Blogger-Radio Host who sold subscriptions for inside information on all the State University athletic teams. They knew the rules; they would have access to coaches and the players, but only "softball" questions were to be asked. If the Network made unexpected visits, the school had final say on what was broadcast. The brand could not be tarnished.

He breathed a sigh of relief every single Friday when each week passed and the cable company trucks and cameramen never appeared in front of the athletic office building. He was certain they would want a statement from him since he was the Chancellor, but no call ever came. He even had the school network's producer use a couple LinkedIn contacts to see what college football shows the Sports Host from the movie cable network might be airing.

The airing of the story did not come in the form of a television show from the movie cable network; it came in a book by the Sports Host. It was only one chapter in a thirty chapter book. It was so devastating and exposing, the Chancellor chewed up two cigars as he read through it. The chapter detailed how football players and star recruits were entertained at strip clubs. It discussed how certain local alumni gave student athletes certain privileges. The job of the Director of Football Operations was to clean up any off-field issues that were caused by the football players. "Make it go away" was the mantra. Thank heavens; the Booster's name was not tied in any way to the mess.

The Chancellor wondered what the motivation was. The Legendary Coach and his Director of Football Operations had been friends. What would motivate the director to turn on the coach and embarrass the university? Was it money? Was there a falling out in the friendship? Did the Director just get sick of it? Now it made sense why the Sports Host was involved. Any other media source would have secretly let him or the AD know. At the end of the day, it really did not matter. The damage was done. The Chancellor did not want to find out the motivating factors of the "former" State University director of football operations.

The alumni and the fans went for blood. It was no surprise that when the book was released, the

Director's condo and his small ranch had already been sold and his cell phone number disconnected. The Athletic Department phones rang non-stop from angry fans. For the first four weeks, the Chancellor's voicemail was full by 10:00 every morning. He knew the Booster's "bark was bigger than his bite," but he still had some concerns the Booster might carry out some of the threats he was saying about the director of football operations

The day the book was released, the Chancellor made a personal call to the Network Executive. They both knew that if the story would gain too much attention, it would damage subscriptions to the University's sports network, increasing The Network's time span to break-even on its investment (third year in a row the university sports network would have major losses). The Network Executive assured the Chancellor the story would not gain momentum. He reminded the Chancellor: The Network is the leader in sports media coverage. The rest of the television and print media follow their lead. If the Network decides there is no story, there is no story.

But both men decided that the Legendary Coach would need to retire before the end of the season. Retirement was the best option, if the university stood behind the coach, it could have severe consequences. There were other national broadcasters beside the Network and they would descend upon the school and be relentless in their coverage. If the Legendary Coach retired, the attention would be on the coach and the new coach they would hire. That would be the story. Anything else would be in the past. Buying out the remainder of the Legendary Coach's contract was no problem.

During the conversation, The Network Executive asked, "Is the plan to promote the offensive coordinator as interim head coach? "

The Chancellor replied, "No, I have someone better."

After a long pause, "Tell me who. We gotta make sure it is well covered when you announce. We'll need time to put together background information."

"I'm hiring the Baptist University coach," the Chancellor said.

"I'll call you once we're a little further along with his agent. Those boys are in the process of winning the conference for the first time." After saying goodbye, he hung up the phone.

"If you can't beat them, join them," he said to no one.

He could feel the smile expand on his face. This hire would solve so many issues. He belted out the once famous expression, "whoa Nelly." So happy, he called the Booster.

"Let's get a drink. I'm buying."

The Reporter
(Mid-Fall 2013, New England)

When the Reporter heard about the chapter in the book, she was already fascinated and intrigued. She really wanted to do a follow-up story. It'd get a cover. There was a bigger story waiting. The Sports Host from the movie cable network was onto something; he had only touched the tip of the iceberg. Most of the viewers of The Network were not readers. If the story was televised, it could reach the masses. The rest of the country, herself included, perceived that Texans were arrogant. She relished the thought of bringing down their egos a notch or two.

The Sports Host had published an article in a national sports magazine in 2009 about the percentage of college football players with criminal records. His data is still used and cited as a resource. It supported the argument for the college football detractors that the game was played by thugs.

She was the investigative reporter. She knew how to uncover the story. She was hired by the Network because of her ability to conduct relentless, productive investigations. Her reputation was rapidly being recognized as the leader in the field.

The Freedom of Information Act (FOIA) had been around before she was born. But in 2007 the law expanded into the Open Government Act, and information about anything related to state and local governments would become available. It was her ticket. She became a student of the Act. She intentionally developed strong relationships with the Network's internal legal department. And while she did not have a Juris Doctorate, she sure knew how to read the law, and she knew how to read files. She was always up for a fight.

She had no concerns that the subject of the chapter was the State University. While she did not care, others within the Network were concerned about going after the State University in fear it could violate the terms of the purchase contract. Before the State University network was purchased, in 2010, the Reporter and the Network sued the State University under the FOIA when rumors of the school leaving the conference began to circulate. She picked up her phone and called the head of the investigative unit of the Network. They had worked together at the morning newspaper in Big D. She knew him well.

"Good morning," the Department Head said. "Something must be on your mind for me to get a call before I've even had my coffee. What's up?".

"Did you see the book? Did you read it?" She asked. She knew he'd know she meant the one about college football written by the Sports Host from the movie cable network.

"I heard about it. You know I spend my day trying to fit two hours of your work into a fifteen minute segment," he teased her. They had known and worked together for a long time both at the Network and at the major paper in Big D, Texas. They had the type of working relationship where they could speak candidly to one another.

"I couldn't put it down. The chapter about the State University players and the strippers is just an inkling of the whole story. I want to cover it," the Reporter said. "There's more here. Can I notify legal that I plan to send out some FOIA requests?"

"You do great work. Let me run it up the flagpole and make sure we get the go ahead," the Department Head said. His cup of coffee would have to wait. He dialed the Network Executive.

Eight hours passed before the reporter saw a text from her producer. It read, "Stand down on this story. U R on the right track. Just pick a different situation/school."

The Commissioner
(Late Fall 2013, Big D, Texas)

The Commissioner of a Power 5 conference has the responsibility to use relationships to stay in front of all breaking new information. He could not believe how easy it was to develop new connections living in Big D. The local society magazine had already done a spread on him after the conference contract was signed with the Network. Texans love football. They love to talk about their favorite teams. They love to share information about their teams.

Often when he was at a restaurant, someone would approach his table, introduce himself, pull up an uninvited chair and start a conversation about football. The subjects ranged from injury reports to recruiting news. The places where the commissioner ate were the same establishments frequented by big money boosters. The bigger the money, the bigger the information the boosters had. The State University had the largest share of boosters, because of the vast numbers of alumni. So the Commissioner was not at all surprised when the Network Executive called him to tell him that the Chancellor was going to make an offer to the Baptist University head coach. He'd been tipped a week before.

Normally, he did not approve of one conference member hiring talent away from another. It created too much animosity and made it almost a zero sum game. But in this case, who cared? To oppose the offer would violate Goal #2. The Commissioner would not deviate from the goal.

Besides, he thought it was ingenious of the Chancellor.

The Baptist University was in the process of winning the conference. It would be their first time. The Baptist University team had beaten the State University team soundly the last couple years. The recruiting class had the appearance of being very good. If the State University was able to sign the Baptist University coach, they would be able to convert his recruits. The Baptist University would sink back to irrelevance and all the other teams could go back to having another easy mark in the win column. They were only graduating three thousand new alumni each year. Any backlash from the hire could be easily managed.

Sitting at the bar of an exclusive Big D club, the Commissioner smiled when his phone vibrated signaling a new text. It was from the Chancellor, "Hope to have big announcement soon. Big day approaching." The Commissioner had envisioned the Chancellor signing off with the university's hand signal, a symbol that had been created decades ago.

He thought to himself, "Too little too late." The fellow sipping on his Macallan two bar stools down had already told him the school was in the market for a new chancellor. The privilege of inside information comes with being the Booster. It was a shame the Chancellor would not be able to enjoy the benefit of the hire.

The Chancellor was one of the first friends the Commissioner made when he accepted the conference position. The Commissioner knew the Chancellor would take it personally and anticipated the Chancellor's disappointment. The Commissioner sent a text to his secretary to buy a box of cigars and dictated a consolatory card. "I was sorry to hear the news. I enjoyed our work together during the conference meetings. I appreciated your input. Much success in your new endeavors, friend."

"Please send to the Chancellor two and a half weeks from today," he added.

The Coach

(Late Fall/Early Winter 2013, Central Texas)

Coach was a pacer. He paced when he talked. He rarely sat down. When his agent called, the first words out of his mouth were, "you better sit down." He was in his seat for one second, and then he shot out of the chair. "How much?" And "How long is the contract?" He paced as he listened to his agent outline the deal.

"Wow. That is one fine offer," the Coach commented.

He took off his hat. He pulled up his sleeves, and then he pushed them back down. He heard his agent talking on the other end of the phone, but he was not listening to a single word. To be offered the head coach position for the State University football team was an honor. Its program had the second most all-time wins in NCAA history. His own son contributed to some of those wins. The entire state of Texas, his home state, took pride in that team. Famous movie stars and country western singers had luxury boxes in the stadium, which was loud. This was the real deal.

"Coach...? Coach, did you hear what I said? Should I tell them OK? I'll have them overnight a set of papers to my office and another to your house..." the agent called out. "This is the job we've been waiting for your entire career, buddy. This is happening."

The words "...waiting for your entire career," echoed in his ear. What the Coach was waiting for was a place that felt like home. What makes a home is a tight family, where each family member has the other's backs. While he lived most of his adult life without a family, Baptist Nation had adopted him. During his journey and time at Baptist University, he developed strong friendships with seven of the Board of Regents' members, along with a couple of the major donors. They were guys like him. They grew up with humble means. They had kicked, scratched, persevered and made successful careers for themselves. But during the new stadium project, they had become even closer. The stadium was about to become a new home to his football team, one they had all built together.

"Coach, do you need more time? A day or two to think things over? Would you like to meet, to talk?" the agent asked.

"No, no, I've made up my mind," Coach responded.

"Great, I'll call the Chancellor at the State University. They are gonna want to coordinate with the media. My sister-in-law is a real estate agent in Capitol City; let's get her to work on finding you that new home. Congrats, Coach."

"I'm staying," he interrupted.

"I want to finish what I've started. I want to keep working with the fellas on the stadium. I want to keep making the team better. No one can stop our spread offense. I have some guys transferring in that will help the defense; we're going to be there. I want to see this Baptist University team compete for a national championship. We are getting close. We made this happen."

"Well, alright, it's your call. I'm not going to talk you out of it. Just pray you don't run out of gas a hundred miles south of Central Texas," the agent joked. It was hard to know whether he was relieved or skeptical about the coach's decision. He didn't know himself whether the Coach had made the right decision.

"Thanks for your help, it means a lot," Coach said. Then he hung up the phone.

He pulled a number from his wallet. A voice on the end said, "Hey, Coach, to what do I owe the pleasure of the call?"

The Coach said, "Let's get the book published about my time here at Baptist University. I want to be here for the long haul. I am ready for us to meet."

Baptist University stepped up and offered the Coach a long term contract. It would take him to the end of his coaching career. The money they offered was very good. The Coach was grateful.

The State University
(Winter 2014, Capitol City, Texas)

When the Baptist University coach did not accept the offer from the State University to become its football coach, it pushed back the timing of the replacement coach. The State University really wanted someone with a Texas background or Texas roots. No household name with a winning streak was available nor were there any disgruntled Texan head coaches in their current position seeking a new opportunity.

The Baptist University had won the conference. The concern to the State University was the momentum they were achieving. The Baptist University head coach had produced a conference championship and a Heisman Trophy winner. The 2014 recruiting class was looking fast, strong and hungry. The State University had to think outside the box for the replacement hire.

The State University hired a man who had been successful at building a star football program at a historically renowned basketball school. Since he was African American, the state school thought it would be advantageously beneficial for recruiting.

What impressed the State University was the coach was a "no nonsense" leader when he ran his football program. What the State University administration and the big money donors did not see coming was how the "no nonsense" attitude translated to "no tolerance" for off the field issues. Over fourteen players were removed from the team. The message was sent. The State University was never again going to provide the subject matter for a book on "off the field" issues of its players.

The Trial – Defensive Player
(Early winter 2014, Central Texas)

The trial of the released defensive player was starting. It had been over a year and a half since charges were pressed. Initially the Defensive Player was going to be tried on five counts of sexual assault. Five women had come forward with alleged assaults involving him. The prosecuting attorney, after hearing their stories, decided to drop the five counts to two. There was one victim, however, that claimed she was assaulted twice. In the other three counts, the prosecuting attorney would use those testimonies as character witnesses.

The Coach had been asked by the Defensive Player if he could say a few words on behalf of the player, but Coach could not honor the request. The Coach asked one of the assistant coaches who was a friend with the local staff writer to find out what was happening in the trial.

The Staff Writer lived near the Baptist University. It was not his alma mater. His indifference to the school made him a good reporter. He could just report the facts without any bias. Because he had been covering the courts for thirty plus years, he was an expert on how each attorney and judge would respond. The juries were more difficult to read.

The Staff Writer got to know the Assistant Coach when a mutual friend invited both men on a deer hunt. Both guys enjoyed hunting, cold beer, and chicken fried steak. Since it was Assistant Coach's turn to buy, they met at Bar and Grill that had been a mainstay in the town for decades. A lot of the Baptist University students would go there on Thursday nights for Fish Bowls of Beer.

Since the Staff Writer did not cover sports, everything was off the record. They chose a table in the restaurant part of the building; it was a corner table in the back. After finishing the last bites of supper and ordering an after dinner beer, the Assistant Coach asked, "How's the trial going? What's your take?"

"It'll be a short one," the Staff Writer said. "Two days, maybe three at the most. Your boy does not have a chance. There was a SANE exam. SANE stands for Sexual Assault Nurse Examiner. These nurses are specially trained to conduct a forensic rape exam. Typically, when an exam is performed, 80% of trial verdicts end up siding with the victim."

The Assistant Coach put his head in his hands and rubbed his cheeks as he was thinking. Every time one of his players "washed out" of the program, he was saddened by the notion that one more life had been wasted by a selfish decision.

"Do you think he did it?" he asked.

"You know what I think doesn't mean a dang thing," replied the Staff Writer. "But, since you asked, I don't think he had consent, but I sure believe *he* thought he had consent. There are some things happening that don't add up."

He stopped to take a sip of beer. "How did your guy end up with a young defense attorney to represent him? You always refer your players to the older attorney."

So basic was the observation, the Assistant Coach didn't know. The Staff Writer was right. The Coach and his staff always referred incidents to the older defense attorney. He was sent everything from underage drinking and speeding tickets to shoplifting and assaults. He did not have an answer. Guessing, he said, "The Defensive Player was kicked off the team before he was arrested. There was no correspondence with him after the arrest. Maybe Judicial Affairs recommended the younger guy? My questions are, Why? Is he doing a terrible job?"

"No," replied the Staff Writer. "He is just missing things, and it hurts his rebuttals and follow-up questions. It appears the preparation was there, but there is a lack of follow-up and questioning. Let's see how he does tomorrow, maybe he will make a comeback."

"I want to come back to this subject, but tell me about the consent," the Assistant Coach urged. He could keep up with the conversation but it took him some time to process what the Staff Writer was saying.

"Do you know what 'talking' is?" asked the Staff Writer leaning back in his chair.

"Yeah, what we are doing now," quickly replied the Assistant Coach.

"Man, I hope not. Talking is what the kids do when they are having casual sex," the Staff Writer continued. "The Defensive Player had just met the alleged victim that night at a party. The victim was a friend of the girl with whom the defensive play was "talking." Let's call her his girlfriend for the sake of conversation. The Defensive Player invited the girlfriend he was banging to the party. He was going to have sex that night. It was a given. The girl he is being accused of sexual assault with was her friend. How does he end up with the girlfriend's friend?"

Guessing, the Assistant Coach said, "There had to be some point during the evening where the girls were not together and the Defensive Player was alone with the alleged victim. Did they get into a fight because the player was hitting on her friend? Did the girlfriend leave because she was jealous? Did the Defensive Player want to have sex so badly with the alleged victim he took her friend outside and assaulted her?"

"Makes sense, except the player and the girlfriend got together later that evening. The victim waited several days before telling the girlfriend her assailant was the player." Leaning forward in his chair and lowering his voice, "The girlfriend's testimony was never presented during the trial."

The Assistant Coach was starting to see the logical progression, "Why wasn't she called as a witness?"

The Staff Writer only shrugged. He didn't have an answer.

It was getting late. They finished their beers. They agreed to meet again the night the verdict came down.

The Assistant Coach lay in bed. His mind was spinning so fast, sleep would be difficult to find. He reflected back to his college days and bachelor's life and even his married life. You never mess with a sure thing. How could the Defensive Player think he had consent? He would wait to call the Coach until he had the whole summary. At this point in his life, he was grateful for his wife and grateful he was married.

The Trial – Defensive Player, Part II
(Early winter 2014, Central Texas)

The Assistant Coach was not sure if it was necessary to meet, since the player was found guilty of two counts of sexual assault and was sentenced to twenty years in prison. The Assistant Coach texted Coach when he first heard the news about the verdict, but the coach had heard as well. The Assistant Coach knew the coach well enough to give him space and time to process the impact of one of his players going to prison. The Staff Writer said they should meet, he had some notes he wanted to share, and they still had to discuss the strangeness of the trial process.

They met again at the same Bar-N-Grill. Each man ordered the "amazing wings," which consisted of jalapeno cheese surrounded by a spherical ball of chicken wrapped in bacon. The Assistant Coach vowed to stick with water so he could keep up with the analytical mind of the Staff Writer, who ordered his beer in a fish bowl and he started the conversation.

"Part of the SANE exam is to have the victim write down all the facts that she can remember. The purpose is that this written testimony will be documented. By completing the exam soon after the assault, it helps the victim record the events. Otherwise, as time goes on, people forget." The Staff Writer took a gulp of beer.

"The prosecuting attorney will use points from that testimony to develop her case. The girl was still "plowed" when she was at the hospital. As you know, drunk people don't make a lot of sense sometimes and are apt to forget, so having the victim write down what happened immediately is even more critical."

"What were the main points?" the Assistant Coach wanted to know.

"The victim said she was gay, she said 'no,' made a comment about his anatomy, and he assaulted her twice. She did not know his full name but referred to him as the girlfriend's man. Don't ask me about the inaccurate descriptions, those are written off because of the alcohol and the trauma."

"It seems cut and dry to me," said the Assistant Coach. "She was underage, went to a party, got drunk, and he took advantage of her. I feel bad for him, and I feel worse for the girl."

"Of course you do! But you went straight to the conclusion. The process that leads to the conclusion is important. The process of this trial is what's out of whack."

The Staff Writer caught the waitress's eye and ordered another beer. The Assistant Coach was staying with his water for now, but allowed his glass to be topped off.

The Staff Writer continued, "The strategy of the defense is to a) prove the high level of intoxication to weaken the victim's credibility, and b) show all the inconsistencies between the victim's story and the Defensive Player's story. The consent piece will always be "he said/she said." The Staff Writer paused to eat another "amazing wing". His attorney only scratched the surface during his questioning."

"Go on," the Assistant Coach leaned forward in his chair.

"Ok, so the amount of alcohol was never challenged. At first it was three cups of trash can punch and two shots of vodka, but the story changed yesterday to two cups of punch and one shot. I doubt the defense attorney was a drinker, three and two or two and one – doesn't matter. Whether you attend school at Baptist University or Party University USA, trash can punch is made with Everclear. Everclear is ninety-five percent alcohol, 190 proof – more than twice the amount of other booze. Plus, the kids drink it out of red Solo cups. Twice the volume size in ounces compared to what you and I can buy at this place or in any bar."

The Staff Writer pulled out his phone, opened an app and showed the coach what the blood alcohol content could have been at 11:00 PM, 2:00 AM, and 4:00 AM.

"Did you show this to the defense?" the Assistant Coach said. He was so fascinated by this conversation that the words came out before he could retract them; he knew how stupid his question was. It was not the beer; it was the situation.

Judging by his friend's embarrassment, the Staff Writer kept his sarcastic comment even keel. "I just report the news buddy, I don't make the news."

"The point is, the defense attorney barely covered the victim's intoxication level. The defense attorney did nothing to attack the character of the victim. He didn't even ask her on the stand whether she knew she was in violation of the Baptist School student policy conduct or Texas underage drinking laws. The questions were shallow at best."

The Assistant Coach nodded his head in silence.

The Staff Writer continued. "The discrepancies in their stories of the night are almost 180 degrees apart. Very few things were agreed by both sides: They both were at the party. The victim drank a lot. The Defensive Player does not drink. They had sex. They were not even in agreement as to how many times they got together," the Staff Writer summarized, then spun his fish bowl for emphasis.

"What were some of the discrepancies?" the Assistant Coach puzzled.

"Who rode with whom to the party? What kind of interaction took place at the party between the alleged victim and the Defensive Player? How they left the party together in order to be alone. The victim claims that a group of her friends arrived at the party in two cars. They stopped and picked up the Defensive Player and took him to the party. She had no interaction with the player whatsoever at the party. The Defensive Player grabbed her by the wrist and led her outside. He then picked her up and carried her to a remote area near the apartment clubhouse and pool area."

"So that is her version. What was *his* story?" asked the Assistant Coach.

The Staff Writer sat forward and responded, "*He* said that they met the victim at the party. He drove to the party with his brother. He said the girls wanted to take pictures with him. The football player said he danced with both girls at the party. He had his brother and another football player testified on his behalf that they saw them dancing at the party. The football player testifies what kind of dancing, gives details, of what was happening on the dance floor, and said the victim started to go down on him during one of the dances. He said they danced four to five songs which could have lasted twenty to twenty-five minutes. The player says she grabbed his hand and led them away from the dancing area. When they got outside, he said she jumped up on him straddling his torso. He said there were three sex incidents, not two.

"So the truth falls somewhere in the middle," the Assistant Coach mused.

"Which is why you bring in witnesses and alibis to verify what happened," the Staff Writer said. "The victim was so adamant that there was no interaction between the two, but the defendant supplied intricate details and had witnesses to the dancing."

"Who cares if it was dancing? Dancing is not the same as sex or sexual assault," defended the Assistant Coach.

"The player said it was booty shaking. Do you know what twerking is?" asked the Staff Writer.

The Assistant Coach looked around the restaurant and nodded his head yes. He wanted to be hip and current, but he was also embarrassed that he knew what twerking was.

"These girls move their pelvic area in sex-like motions. They will straddle the guy's leg and rub against it like they are having sex. Or the guy will be behind the girl and press himself against her ass like they are having sex. It's -- it's -- extremely provocative for those dancing, and onlookers.

The Assistant Coach interrupted, "Let me guess: The defense attorney did not describe to the jury the type of dancing. So even if a juror was familiar with twerking, the erotic nature of the dancing was not described in detail?"

"Correct," said the writer. "So the prosecuting attorney made it a point to address the issue by emphasizing to the jury that nothing the girl and the football player did prior to the sex had any significance as to whether sexual assault occurred. She also made it seem to the jury that the two witnesses who saw the couple dancing, were making it up. By accusing the witnesses of lying about the dancing, she was able to discredit their testimonies."

"But what happens before the sex, does have significance, correct?," questioned the assistant coach.

The Staff Writer concluded, "If the player was dancing with the girl, and she was straddling his leg rubbing against him, the player would have gotten turned on. If he's dancing with a hard-on and the girl knows it, and proceeds to want to go down on him in front of everyone at the party, the player might think he has consent. But we'll never know because it just wasn't addressed in court."

"But if there were 50-100 kids there, who all have cell phones, surely someone took a picture?" Assistant Coach wondered.

"You would think, but once again the topic never came up during the trial. Not once," the Staff Writer again replied.

"While it makes sense, it is just theoretical. No one could prove it," the Assistant Coach said.

"Correct," agreed the Staff Writer. "It was a ballsy move to put any defendant on the stand. So much can go wrong. The picture of what happened gets even murkier when I tell you that thirty minutes are missing from the security video of the complex where the party was held. This missing segment showed the pool area where the sexual acts occurred. It gets even weirder when I tell you that the Defensive Player had a minute long video on his cell phone of him and the girl leaving the party and heading to the first place they had sex."

The Assistant Coach almost choked on the bite of chicken and bacon he had in his mouth. "What? Missing? A video? Who would have tampered with a security video?"

The Staff Writer continued, "Once again, it was never brought up. The player's video was dark and the audio was hard to hear. He had sent it to a family member, who had it enhanced and added subtitles so you make out what was being said." The player and his attorney waited until the trial started to present it as evidence. Maybe for the drama or impact, but the judge and the prosecutor were ticked off about not receiving it earlier."

"Wouldn't video be enough evidence for the player to support his version of the story?" asked the Assistant Coach.

"No. The prosecuting attorney did a superb job of claiming the video was produced later on a different night - not the night the sexual assaults occurred," explained the Staff Writer.

"But his phone would have had the date of the video, correct"? The Assistant Coach wanted affirmation to his statement.

"That was the point made by the prosecuting attorney. And when she questioned the player about the phone there was an incredible awkwardness in the courtroom. The player had been calm, cool, and collected throughout the last two days. He was polite, factual in his answers, remained under control even when the prosecuting attorney was in his face. But when she asked why he didn't give the phone or video to Judicial Affairs… I mean, it could have been his ticket out of the situation. He was stumped. He looked over at his attorney for help, and any momentum he had gained during the trial was completely gone," the Staff Writer said.

The men finished their meals. They asked for the check and sat in silence. As they waited, the Staff Writer leaned back and said, "Ok, off the record, did you, or Coach, or any of the coach's friends pay for the Defensive Player's legal counsel?" asked the Staff Writer.

The Assistant Coach had known the Coach for a long time. He had followed him during his career and had been on staff with the coach at his last three stomping grounds. He had never known the Coach to pay for any bail, counseling, ticket, or legal advice (although he made referrals and introductions). After processing the question, he replied, "No." And then, "Was that really eating at you?"

"No, but your telling me that eliminates one of the possibilities. If the football staff was not involved, it says to me that the University wanted him gone. Somehow a deal was struck to allow him to transfer to another school after you kicked him off the team. I know you help players who wash out, land elsewhere with other programs so they don't miss a year. The school had no interest in letting the player present neither his case nor his video to Judicial Affairs. The school was content to let the situation play out legally in court," concluded the Staff Writer.

The check came, and they paid it in silence, both deep in thought.

The men shook hands and got into their respective trucks. Unintentionally, they had parked next to each other. The Staff Writer signaled the Assistant Coach to roll down his window. He raised his voice to be heard over the running engines and said, "One more thing: One of the witnesses blew off her appointment she was supposed to have with a police officer. She never returned the officer's calls and it appears she got a new phone or at the very least a new phone number. A police officer was called to testify on the stand," started the Staff Writer before he was interrupted.

"Same officer on both cases?" asked the assistant coach.

"No, different ones," answered the Staff Writer. "But after she gave her testimony of what transpired, the prosecuting attorney 'bitch slapped' the police officer. She demeaned the officer asking why the police department didn't come directly to the district attorney and utilize the power of a grand jury. A message was sent. A strong message was sent from the DA's office to the PD. You better Google "grand juries." The power of prosecution without charges being pressed is a game changer for police reports; I'm already late getting home."

He was going to text Coach, but decided to call instead. The call went immediately to voicemail. He left the following message: "Coach, lot of info to discuss with you; let me know when we can meet. It will make your head hurt. Man, these players sure have a different college experience than we did in school."

The Assistant Coach forgot to look up the impact and influences of a grand jury. He didn't even know which states permitted grand juries, so the information was never relayed to the Coach.

One month after the meeting between Staff Writer and the Assistant Coach, the municipal police department submitted a new file to the District Attorney for a Grand Jury. The file contained a case about another football player. It involved a transfer football player that never played a down for the Baptist University who was accused of sexual assault. The player was never listed on the roster since he had to sit out a year.

Ironically, the Baptist University would be conducting its internal investigation of the incident, with Judicial Affairs handling the process. It would be determined the Transfer Player would not be found guilty of sexual assault by the University. The alleged victim ended up transferring to another school.

The Reporter
(Spring 2014, New England)

It was only a minor setback for her career and her personal ambitions to be unable to investigate in detail what had happened in Capitol City, Texas. The Reporter had something even better. She knew about a project that just had been approved by the head of the investigative news department would meet some resistance from the Network Executive. She knew it would ultimately be cleared because the fan reaction to the project would be immense.

The basis of the project was to use public records and determine if college football players were given preferential treatment when they were involved in criminal activity compared to criminal activity of similarly aged college kids who don't play ball. She presented a list of ten schools to the Department Head. Twenty letters of Freedom of Information Act requests were about to be sent. Ten letters would be sent to the police departments of the schools; ten letters would be sent to the police departments of the municipal cities where the universities were located.

The Department Head and the Network Executive had to sign off on her choices. They wanted to make sure that the Network favorites were not on the list. Also, they would prohibit any school that could affect the Network's bottom line profits. The Reporter decided that the ten schools had to be a sampling of each of the Power 5 conferences. They had to be in states that were liberal in disclosing and releasing information requested under the FOIA. She was also looking for schools that had had headline stories of assault in the last two years.

Florida schools were her first choice, because the state of Florida allowed background checks on minors to be performed. She also researched the Office of Civil Rights to see which schools were under investigation for Title IX infractions. The first nine were fairly easily chosen. Her tenth university chosen was the most controversial. Part of her decision to include it was personal.

The Catholic University was the final school added; it had a sexual assault case in 2012. She heard from one of her sources that the Catholic University was one of the universities cited in a movie documentary about college rapes. The most tragic event occurred because the victim, who was a student at a school near the Catholic University, committed suicide in part because she felt no one believed she had been sexually assaulted.

The Reporter had lost someone very dear in her life as well. It was a void that she would hold the rest of her days. There was a pain she knew would never go away. Her reasons were easy to justify.

Even though she was Catholic herself, she was not a religious person. Growing up in the Midwest, she would attend mass at Easter and Christmas and maybe once or twice more during the year just to please her mother.

She never went to confession. Why bother? She was unsure if God existed. If so, then why did he not answer her prayers when she needed Him most? But if God did exist and He allowed her loved one to die then He must be cruel. So a little payback would be good for her well-being and the family of the deceased victim. When she licked the final envelope closed, she said, "I'll show you," unsure if the comment was for Catholic University or for God.

The State University and the Baptist University

(Summer 2014, Central Texas and Capitol City, Texas)

In the summer of 2014, two news stories were announced about football players at State University and Baptist University. The former received national attention where two State University football players were charged with sexual assault of a female student. The other story was just a blip in the local headlines about how a transfer football player, who never played a down and was never on the roster, was indicted for sexual assault.

Ninety-nine percent of the general public thinks that "charged" and "indicted" mean the same thing. Twenty-three states in America have Grand Juries: Texas is one of them. A grand jury is a jury that hears all the facts from just the prosecution and decides if there is enough evidence to indict. Charges do not have to be pressed by the victim. So the outcome of due process and the verdict determines the decision making process for all the parties who have an interest in the case. Prosecutors work with Grand Juries to decide to bring criminal charges against potential defendants. Typically, a judge is not present and they are not open to the public.

Grand Juries are kept in strict confidence. They are designed for witnesses to speak freely without any possibility of retaliation. If a Grand Jury chooses to indict, the trial process moves faster. The prosecutor does not have to prove to a judge there is enough evidence to go to trial.

The Coach
(Early December 2014, Central Texas)

The season flew by for the Coach. The opening of the new stadium was monumental. Attending a Baptist University football game became an experience. Fans and students filled the parking lots and open spaces hours before each home game. Alumni and fans were taking boats to get to the stadium which was on a river. Tailgating now included "sailgating." The Baptist alumni were free to have adult drinks before the game, while the campus remained dry; they no longer had to hide small pints of whiskey in their boots.

Behind one of the end zones was a well-cut, manicured berm where fans could sit. The Coach remembered asking "what the Sam Hill is a berm?" two years ago when the idea was first presented to him. He originally thought it had to do with a triangle or a pair of plaid shorts.

The 2014 season marked the first time where the college football system had a play-off in place. Their conference was the only conference without a championship game since it still needed two more schools to join. The NCAA required conferences to have at least twelve teams to have a championship game. To counter the NCAA requirement, the Commissioner had the idea to run ads stating that there was only one champion since all the teams played each other. It made sense, and every team thought the Commissioner's idea was a good one and voted in favor of it at the conference meeting.

The season had one game remaining; the Baptist University football team did not occupy one of the top four ranking spots. It was hovering in the two national polls at #5 and #6. Depending on the poll, the number #4 spot was held by the Private University in the conference and THE University in Ohio.

Typically when a game is over and the Coach's team loses, he forgets about the loss. He moves on. The Coach's attitude was that the past was the past. It can't be changed. He would then divert all his thinking and energy to the next game.

A loss to the Coal Miner State University was the biggest obstacle that was preventing his team from going to the college playoffs. His team was built for speed and for hundred degree days in the hot Texas sun. The Coal Miner State University game was an away game. The cold and dampness of the West Virginia air was like putting sand into a well-oiled machine. Because of scheduling, The Network had scheduled the game at 11:00 in the morning. His team incurred over 200 yards of penalties. The home team had nowhere near that amount of penalized yards, but Coach learned long ago never to say anything derogatory about the officiating.

What chapped his backside were the seven pass interferences calls his defensive backs were flagged for committing. Some of the officiating calls were legitimate but a couple of particularly untimely calls seemed to favor the home team. The Coach really wanted him to check the drivers' licenses for residency of the officiating crew. While his team battled, the offensive turnovers prevented the game from being even close.

That loss continued to haunt him. His team would have been undefeated. The Baptist University team would have been one of the top four teams. They would have been in the college playoffs.

The good news was that there was only one more game left in the season. It was home. If they won, his football team would be back to back conference champions. Even though its record would be tied with another team in the conference, the Baptist University team would be the champion because they had beaten the Private University at home earlier in the year. The Baptist University team would win the tie-breaker.

Coach decided once again just to focus on the game at hand. He could not control the selection process of the college committee that would choose the four teams. He still liked their chances even though the national media was complaining about his team's weak non-conference schedule. But he knew the Commissioner of the conference was loyal to the conference. The Coach knew the Commissioner had ties to people on the selection committee. He knew the Commissioner wanted the conference represented in the playoffs.

What he *did not* know was that the Commissioner had zero loyalty and zero fondness for the Baptist University and its head coach.

The Commissioner
(December 2014, Big D, Texas)

The conference couldn't hold a championship game because it didn't have enough teams. NCAA by-laws mandated that a conference must have at least twelve schools. The Network Executive had made it crystal clear to the Commissioner not to add two new teams. College football as an industry was hotter than ever. However, subscriptions to the Network were down and the Network continued to lose money on the purchase of the State University network. It was the fourth year in a row. If the Commissioner added two more teams to his conference, the Network would have to pay out to each of the new teams, the same amount of money they were paying to the existing teams. Each team in the conference was getting over twenty-two million dollars a year.

As he sat his desk, he reviewed all the season statistics for all the teams one more time. Three of the top places for the college football playoffs were locks. Three of the other conferences were already represented. This left three viable teams competing for the final play-off spot. All three of these teams would have the same record. Two of the three teams were teams in his conference. However, those two teams were being scrutinized by the national media for having weak non-conference games.

As it stood, one of the conference teams was ranked #4; the other was ranked #6. Insiders on the college playoff selection committee told the Commissioner that the committee was leaning toward the fourth spot coming from the Northern conference. THE University in Ohio, ranked #5 at the time, had a history of winning seasons and the historic ability to recruit blue chip players. Insiders told him that the team from the Northern conference's only loss was a fluke upset from a non-conference opponent. If they had a win on the last game of the season, they would jump up into the fourth spot. The insiders told him that there was only a small chance that minds would be changed.

The Commissioner decided that a small chance was better than no chance at all. He looked at the scores and opponents of all the games from the Private University and the Baptist University. The Private University had beaten a team from the Northern Conference in one of its non-conference games. Even though the Private University lost to the Baptist University, they lost to them by only three points, on the road, and had dominated the Baptist team three of the four quarters. He called the presidents of the two large state schools just to get their opinions. It was his decision, but he was still following Goal #2: Keep both schools happy. Neither of them was in the running, but making the call to them anyway was a wise move. They reminded him of a conference rule that permitted ties.

It looked like the three contenders would win their last games. He was not a religious man, and praying was not a part of his life. But if there were such things as football gods, he was hoping the Baptist University and the school from the Northern conference would lose. He slapped his desk out of frustration. He made up his mind.

If one of the insiders, media personnel, or anyone on the selection committee asked his opinion, he would voice his support for the Private University. Even though the conference advertised as having only one champion, if both schools won their final game, he would announce both as Co-Champions.

He knew there would be a backlash. The Baptist University was playing a top ten ranked conference foe. The backlash would be small. The Commissioner could handle the backlash. He justifiably thought The Baptist University was fortunate enough to even be in the conference, let alone winning it back to back in football.

As he looked out the window of his office he was still somewhat surprised how warm the Big D, Texas winters were. He collected a few file folders and locked them in his desk. "No one cares about the Baptist University. I sure don't give damn about them," were his last thoughts. His decision was final.

The Coach

(After the final game of 2014 season, Central Texas)

"Co-Champions? Co-Champions," said the bewildered coach, but he couldn't even hear himself. The stadium was booing at a noise level equal to the cheering applause just an hour before. The air was thick with a deafening roar of unhappiness. The Coach was caught off guard that the first emotion he felt was hurt, betrayal. His knees actually buckled under him as he removed his headset. All his life he had been able to suppress anger. He would suppress it long enough to cover it with his Texan whimsical charm. It was his gift to diffuse tense situations with humor. It was the charm that endeared fans to him. It was wit that caused his players to be loyal to him. Not this time. He saw the Commissioner holding the trophy. A trophy that he would be forced to share with a team they had beaten. No way. Mercy had left the building. He had some choice words burning on his tongue that needed to be said.

In Texas, when you insult another man's manhood, you are asked to step outside. When you are outside in front of 45,000 people, there are no written rules to follow. The only saving grace was the microphone was not turned on when the Commissioner presented the trophy to the Coach. The fans that filled the stadium did not hear the verbal venom from the Coach. The Commissioner had the advantage because he had prepared himself for the coach's anger. He quietly whispered to the coach, "I hope you don't live to regret those words." The Commissioner was not going to forgive and he sure as hell was not going to forget.

As the Coach received the trophy, he announced to the packed stadium, "Baptist University is the only conference champion," as he glared at the Commissioner. "If we are going to have a conference slogan, let's stick with it. Don't say one thing and then do another. That is my issue."

The Coach continued, "I'm not obligated to the conference. I'm not obligated to the Commissioner. I am obligated to Baptist University and our football team. We are part of the conference; we have been champions for the last two years and the conference needs to be obligated to us because we are making the conference image better throughout the country."

The crowd erupted so loud that the ground crew was concerned the fans might tear down the goalposts. The Commissioner's face burned with an artificial smile he was faking. He said to himself, "Big mistake, Coach."

During the next week, neither of the conference teams made the playoffs. The team from the Northern conference filled the last spot. The Commissioner kept his comments to the media brief and tersely expressed his disappointment but he knew the selection committee had tough choices to make. Coach, on the other hand, was vocal about not having enough representation from people in the South.

The Reporter
(December 24, 2014, New England)

She knew she would get the full spectrum of push back from the ten different schools and police departments. Some of the information rolled in quickly from the police departments, other departments were slow and stalled their responses. When all was said and done, she had over 2,000 documents to review.

It was the day before a holiday. She told her husband she was just going to work a few hours in the morning. The Reporter needed to start compiling and reviewing some of the information she'd received. By noon, she called home and said she was running late. She quickly went through her emails and sent out a couple tweets. She compiled some stats, and ran some of the information she'd received against online police record websites.

A "couple more hours" turned into nearly a full day. She was getting ready to turn off her laptop and commute home when her computer "dinged," signaling new email. She knew better than to look, but she was curious to see who else was working as hard on a holiday.

The Scapegoat

Twenty emails were in her inbox; most had subject lines that resembled quotes from the movie, Scarface. Because her investigative work sometimes centered on sexual assaults, the Network's IT department had very few filters for her emails. The Reporter was not surprised that so many emails made their way through into her inbox.

She called her husband to tell him she was finally on her way and noticed eight new voicemails and twenty-one new texts. None of the numbers matched up to contacts in her phone and were from all over the United States. The largest concentration was in Florida.

She only had to read one email and one text to figure out someone had put her email address and cell phone number online. The messages were all the same: folks in Florida were angry that The Reporter wanted information about their football and basketball players. "Who posted my personal information?" she asked herself, shaking her head. She knew there would be enemies when she took on this project. She was so absorbed with the thoughts of her personal information being posted and concerned if she might need protection that she almost ran three red lights on her commute home.

Later that evening, as she was sipping her "good night" glass of merlot, she got onto the internet. Her husband had been asleep for an hour and the last present had been wrapped and bowed twenty minutes ago. Investigative searches were her expertise. It only took one Google search to find out who posted her personal information. One of the police departments in Florida posted a copy of her letter along with all the information she requested. All three hundred names of the requested athletes and all the information related to them were there. If the Florida police department was going to make the FOIA information available for the Network, it was going to make it available to everyone.

"Merry Christmas, assholes," she said. She did not gain her position and reputation by being scared or intimidated. It came with the territory. The Reporter had already prepared her legal department for the battle. She was ready for a long fight. She was prepared to file lawsuits. If those failed, the Reporter was prepared to appeal any verdict that was unfavorable to her and the Network. The 2,000 pieces of information were covering three years' worth of stories.

The Reporter was smart enough not to respond to any of the texts, emails, or phone calls. She didn't feel baited; it wasn't her fight. She had the power of the pen. The Reporter had the Freedom of Information Act behind her. She had tenacious attorneys that would help litigate the way to receive the desired information. She would develop and create the stories that would come from the information. The Reporter could deliver a story that had impact.

Closing her eyes in bed, she wished she could see the expression on the face of "I hope U die C- word@

gmail.com," when he read the article in six months about his beloved football team and school.

Pulling up the covers, she whispered, "But I heard him exclaim, ere he drove out of sight, Merry Christmas to all, are you ready to fight?

The Reporter knew 2015 was going to be a great year.

The Network Executive
(Summer 2015, New England)

The Network Executive excelled at making and keeping allies. He had built a strong professional bond with the Chancellor at the State University. When the Chancellor "retired", he agreed to remain one more year until the new chancellor became acclimated to the position. The Chancellor no longer had any power and he was no longer of use to the Network Executive. The new chancellor was ex-military. His personality matched the personality of the new State University head coach; it was going to take a while for the Network Executive to build a rapport. In order to protect his investment, his new allies were the big time Booster and Blogger-Radio Host located in Capitol City.

The Network Executive had known the Blogger-Radio Host for a long time. He was considered an ally to the Network because of his friendships with so many of the Network employees. The Network Executive described his friend as a blueblood with a lot of connections. The radio talk host/blogger graduated from Rich Kid University and had made a lot of deep pocket friendships there. Deep pocket friendships meant ties with people who had influence to go along with their affluence. He had spent the first twenty years of his career covering sports at the multinational nonprofit press agency and the largest newspaper in Big D. He was a go-getter with a nose for finding the "juice" behind good stories. He made sure he stayed in contact with former co-workers.

The other key ally for the Network Executive was the Booster. The Booster was a mega-wealthy individual with good relationships in business, government, and even church when necessary. The Booster knew the Blogger-Radio host. The Booster listened to the radio show in the morning. He was a subscriber to the blog, although he never posted in fear that his identity might be revealed. He was the type of man who would return phone calls, but rarely initiated them because he had everything he already wanted. People came to him.

So, when the Network Executive's phone vibrated, he was surprised to see that it was the Booster.

"Hello," answered the Network Executive who was sitting at his desk.

"I have some news that is going to make your day!" the Booster shouted through the phone. "You are gonna feel like you just won the Super Bowl and you're headed to Disneyworld!"

It had been a rough summer for the Network Executive. The Reporter had written her article about criminal activity among college athletes. Each of the conference commissioners politely called to go on the record so that they could report back to each of the schools that were in the article about how they vehemently opposed the article. A couple of the schools that had huge fan bases and some of the staff employees that were alumni of the schools voiced their frustration about the article. For every school that complained, there were ten others that just saw their recruiting efforts get ten percent easier. The Booster loved the article because one of the subject schools was an in-state rival in a different conference and another one was in his conference.

"I could use some good news," said the Network Executive. He could hear music in the background from the Booster but the Network Executive could not determine whether the Booster was calling from one of his vacation homes or his ranch. The location really did not matter the Booster was clearly celebrating.

"The Texas Senate will be voting this summer to pass a state Freedom of Information Act that will apply to private institutions. It means that all notes from meetings may be subject to public view. It puts those bastards on the same level playing field as the state schools and public universities."

The Network Executive was not about to argue the fine points of a level playing field. The State University had plenty of competitive advantages. He did not respond.

The Booster continued, "This means all the private universities including the hypocritical Baptist University will be held accountable. So *we* or should I say our media friends should be able in the future request budgets, contracts, any information that may be of value." The Booster was giddy with excitement.

The Network Executive considered this.

"How do you know it will pass? It seems like something your political party would not endorse or vote on," replied the Network Executive.

"Politics? This isn't about politics. This is about football," said the Booster. "Plus, tomorrow a group of my friends will be making some campaign donations. I like sure things," said the Booster. Laughing at his own joke, he said, "Enjoy Disneyworld! Tell Mickey the eyes of Texas are on him!" The noise of a margarita being blended drowned out the Booster's good-bye.

The Writer

(Early August 2015, Capitol City, Texas)

Texas has a rich cultural history of being Republican except for the Capitol City. Feminists, environmentalists, homosexuals and other liberals have found Capitol City a great place to congregate and live. T-Shirts and bumper stickers reinforce keeping the city weird. It is Texas and all Texan Democrats and Republicans love their football. Those who live in Capitol City love the State University football team.

The Writer had moved to Capitol City from Florida to pursue a doctorate from the State University. Her work appeared in some national feminist publications as well as several local Texas journals. The Network's magazine and the national sports magazine were publishing more of her articles in their women's section. Although she had only contributed to other friends' books, her very own was in the works. She was a mystery to her friends, however, because they had trouble accepting the fact that she was a feminist at all – she did not fit the stereotype. She was an attractive blond who knew college football in every direction, more so than avid male fans.

But her passion for the game burned out when a sexual assault case surfaced a few years ago at her alma mater.

She was so enraged at how the assault was handled by university officials and the local Florida media. She thought the focus was so centered on trying to clear the player (since it occurred before the professional football draft); the victim, on the other hand, was all but prevented telling her side of the story on what happened. This tragedy shifted her passion for the game to the passion of holding university officials responsible for sexual assaults on their campuses.

On a hot August day, a group of the Writer's friends were enjoying mexi-tinis and one another's conversation at a downtown rooftop bar. Capitol City was the popular upbeat place to hang out. Around the table sat a gay software developer who owned his own company and a director of nursing who was in town for the week visiting friends.

The conversation turned to football and it didn't take long for the conversation to turn to the State University Team and how it would fare in 2015. They each gave opinions about the head coach, starting new players and the recruiting class. Then, the Director of Nursing mentioned conference rivals. He complained, "We have to play the Baptist University away this year; I can't stand those guys."

The Software Developer quickly chimed, "I hate the coach. He reminds me of everything Texas stood for in the 50's. He's such a throwback. Arrogant and pompous. I can't believe a high school football coach has had the success he has had.

"Why would anyone play for him?" asked the Writer.

The Software Developer once again had a quick answer. "It's because he's a second chance guy. He recruits thugs. Thugs who have sketchy pasts. Thugs who are still criminals. He thinks that football is the way out for them like it was when he was in college. He's a diehard Texan."

"What do you mean about his players being criminals?" asked the Director of Nursing.

The Software Developer replied, "I once made a list of all the questionable characters he's recruited and what happened to them after they joined his program. I have data on fifteen or so players. I am happy to show it to you. I'll upload it to Google docs. You might like it. Hey, I was wondering how I could put dirt to good use."

"Interesting," said the Director of Nursing. "I'm from West Texas and back home there's a lot of rumor and speculation about how he got the 'five star' quarterback to commit. I'd love to see it."

"I'll shoot over an email letting you know when it is online and ready for download," the Software Developer stated.

"Why haven't you sent it to all the message boards to get some traction?" the Director of Nursing asked.

"I guess I've been waiting for the right moment," returned the Software Developer.

The Scapegoat

The right moment was less than three weeks away.

On the way back to her office, the Writer's phone vibrated with a text. When she got to her desk, she took out the phone and stared at the text. It read, "You are welcome! There is a sexual assault case going to trial in Central Texas. It's under the radar screen. Player's name XXXXX. You don't owe me. But you're welcome."

The number was in her contacts. She wouldn't necessarily call him a friend. He was an attorney who was on the same side of Title IX as the Writer. They had gotten to know each other when a famous player at a Florida University was accused of sexual assault. The attorney, of course, represented the victim and was filing lawsuits against the school. She started her own Google searches. Within minutes, she found the player's information.

She called a friend who had a background and expertise for tearing through information in state court records. She told him to drop what he was doing. They were getting ready to make a road trip and she was going to pick him up in ten minutes. She was not the only person to whom the attorney would send a tip. She knew of two others: one from California and the other, New York. She was an hour and half away; the others would have to catch planes, then have layovers in order to puddle jump to central Texas. The race was on to break the story.

As she drove, she assumed the attorney would be representing the victim in any civil matters. When they arrived at the courthouse and learned that a judge had put a gag order on the case, she knew the attorney needed her to break the story. The attorney knew that the more media attention a case received, the larger the settlement. She didn't mind being used, this was the best information she'd received in a long, long time. And it was all hers.

Second Trial – Transfer Player
(Mid -August 2015, Central Texas)

Out of courtesy, the Staff Writer called his friend the Assistant Coach and asked if he needed to meet again. "There is a fish bowl beer with your name on it," he teased.

"No, I'm jammed with the new season starting in three weeks. The Coach really likes our chances this year. This trial's really a distraction. Just keep me posted if there is something I should know," the Assistant Coach said.

"Do you have a twitter account?" asked the Staff Writer. "I'll be posting live the next couple days" he paused before asking, "Are you ok?"

"I'm fine. This kid never played a down for us. He wasn't even on the roster. He was another second chance kid, but this time it didn't work. He used up his chances."

"Coach is feeling the pressure" the Assistant Coach added. "I've got to run. I'll keep an eye on my Twitter feed. By the way, the kid is represented by the older defense attorney. They called my office after the indictment. I recommended him."

"Yep, I saw his name on the docket," replied the Staff Writer. "Hang in there, amigo."

The Assistant Coach watched his phone over the next few days. He was aware of most of the facts since Judicial Affairs had already internally investigated the situation. It was a thorough discovery period, but in the end the Transfer Player was cleared. The coaching staff thought the transfer player would be able to play football.

As he followed the trial on this phone over the next few days, he learned a few new facts. The woman had had a rape examination. The Transfer Player and the victim were friends. There was a history of messing around. Unlike the trial involving the Defensive Player, the stories of the Transfer Player and the victim were almost the same. The only difference was whether the sex was consensual.

The Assistant Coach never gambled. But if he was a betting man, he figured the player had no chance. What was it he'd heard? Eighty percent of all trials turn into convictions if a rape exam is performed.

The Assistant Coach got a text from the Staff Writer announcing the trial was over. "The jury is out. Transfer Player sent damning texts to the victim. His texts stated that what happened between them was not rape. The DA destroyed the credibility of his roommate, and the ex-girlfriend from his old school who testified about assaults she had experienced with him. It's over."

And then, "Hey, FYI – the media is all over the place, and they all wanna know if Coach knew about the Transfer Player's violent past."

The Boom – The Writer
(Mid-August 2015, Capitol City Texas)

Boom! She did it. She broke the story in the Statewide Periodical immediately after the Transfer Player's verdict had been released. She had never worked so hard and produced such good work in such a short period of time. It was powerful. She was able to convey the story without making it personal. She made the point to every reader. How much did the head coach know about the Transfer Player's history? Why was the coaching staff so confident the player would return to the team?

She turned on her laptop to reread the article. She settled down on her couch with coffee warming her hands and a State University logo blanket covering her legs. Even though it was summer, she liked keeping the house air conditioned. The comments section in the online edition was on fire. The Baptist University haters were in back and forth heated banter with the Baptist University fans. She could not have scripted a better scenario. The comments were great entertainment.

Then she saw *the* comment. She did not recognize the moniker, but it was the Software Developer. Her friend posted all his research on the questionable characters recruited by the Baptist University head coach. Even the

Baptist fans were taken aback. Mainstream media was like an air assault attack: lots of damage, few casualties. Social media is the boots on the ground, and in the trenches. The comment by the Software Developer's posting was powerfully damaging.

The comment included background information and "off the field" problems of fifteen Baptist University football players. The problems ranged from drug usage to sexual assault. The comment claimed one common factor – all the players were recruited by the Coach. Because the Software Developer documented the sources of some of the information, it was evident he had been documenting this information for a long time.

The Writer made a couple Google searches on the Software Developer's "questionable character research" posting. It was already on message boards of over half the schools in the conference. "Wow, that was faster than I predicted," she whistled. Readers had seen the comment and were posting it all over the internet. Her article was fair, and it was poignant. While she did not believe there was any spin to her article; she was under no obligation to print a counterpoint. She had legitimate questions for the Baptist University officials.

The message boards took her position of questioning the school's officials, but the communication made a quantum leap. The boards were targeting just one of the Baptist University officials – the Coach. The people that posted on the boards were mean spirited. Some of the postings were vulgar. Profanity was common. But the underling hatred for the Coach and the Baptist University was surprising.

Twenty-four hours later, the Software Developer's "questionable characters" posting was on every school in the conference. It was being cut and pasted on other Division I message boards all over the country. Wow. She was a little concerned because her friend made a pedophile reference on the recruiting of one of the coach's players. This was such a hot button issue because of what happened to a school in the east, she felt a stab of panic. Any time the word "pedophile" is used – it can be damning. She was concerned that particular comment had no evidence to support it.

The Writer reminded herself that she couldn't say for sure it was her friend who posted it. It was in the comment section and could never be traced back to her. Any reader could post a comment. It did not matter whether the reader knew the Writer personally. No one would be able to know. She finished her coffee and put the empty mug on the floor. She lightly punched one of the pillows on the couch and contemplated for a moment. Her only regret was that she wished the trial of the Transfer Player had occurred two months earlier. She was finishing her book and all her hard work could only be added at the very end. Had the trial been earlier, she would have included the information in more of the chapters.

The Coach
(Mid-August, 2015, Central Texas)

The 2015 team looked to be the best he'd ever had. He had great starting and back-up quarterbacks, powerful and explosive receivers, veteran offensive linemen, and athletic, reliable receivers. The plan was to outscore other teams. His mind was filled with plays and new plays and scoring touchdowns. The only trouble was figuring out how to distribute the football among so much talent. It was a good problem to have.

The trial of the Transfer Player was a huge distraction. "What the Sam Hill?" the Coach said to himself. Of course, the other school's head coach hadn't shared with him the alleged violent assaults the Transfer Player had made on his girlfriend. "Dang. That conversation I had with the other coach was over two and a half years ago, and he told me nothing. Not one thing," though he knew as he said it that it wouldn't matter. The media would assume he knew. They'd expect his memory to recall it as if it happened yesterday.

"Think, think, think what was said?," he asked himself as he removed his ball cap and rubbed his hand over his head. He remembered the other coach saying the player was depressed. He remembered the player was homesick for Texas. Heck, what Texan wouldn't be?

The Coach continued to ask himself, "Girlfriend? Was there a girlfriend? A honey, anything? Babymama? Girl?" And then, Yes! He remembered the other coach saying it was 'rocky,' and their relationship might be the cause of the depression. Did he mention hitting her? Strangling her? No Way! "Rocky relationship...," he had said. The Coach would have remembered any physical violence that was for sure. Drugs? Drugs sounded vaguely familiar, but if someone was potentially suicidal, taking drugs (prescription or illegal) would make sense to a distressed player. He wanted to see if there was any documentation that might jog a memory. The Transfer Player's former coach was telling the media that all of the details of the Transfer Player's behavior had been told to The Coach. That claim was untrue.

The Coach called the Assistant Coach. He told the Assistant Coach to call Judicial Affairs and Compliance and see what documentation they had on the Transfer Player. Both departments kept records. The Coach did not want to call anyone a liar but he sure as Sam Hill did not want to be called one either.

The Coach was firm on the following: The Transfer Player never played a down for the Baptist University. He was not on the roster. The school had performed an extensive investigation. The kid even passed a lie detector test, and had witnesses.

The Assistant Coach called back in a few days. "Coach, the only document that Compliance had was a copy of the Transfer Information sheet from an email. I made a copy if you need it. Everything else has been boxed up and sent over to Judicial Affairs per their instructions."

The Assistant Coach continued, "I don't know if it helps but the Transfer Player's school visit was over a week before we received the transfer request, which was the end of the month. He was dismissed from his old team after the first week in May. That only gave the kid two weeks to contact us and two other schools. He had to set up his visits. He still had to pass his finals. His grades would have had to be turned in on the day he visited us. It sure doesn't seem like a lot of time, so it is likely that your conversation would have been in April. Especially since we knew the kid did not suit up for the spring game. We know he wasn't physically hurt."

The Coach hopefully, asked, "Do we have a copy of the Permission to Contact letter?" This was the NCAA guideline letter a transferring player would have to complete and sign to be able to talk to new schools about the possibility of playing for them.

"Coach, I doubt it. If we did, it is in a box in Judicial Affairs," the Assistant Coach told him. "By the way, Judicial Affairs has battened down the hatches. They told me they don't have time to answer my questions or help supply any information. The Baptist University President is demanding to know how the verdict from the Transfer Player's trial concluded something completely different from the school's internal investigation. He's pissed. Judicial Affairs is pissed."

The wedge between the Judicial Affairs and the athletic department was being driven deeper and deeper. Two weeks later, the in-house counsel for the Baptist University made a recommendation to hire an outside law firm to investigate. The investigative process would take nearly a year.

The Blogger-Radio Host
(Late August 2015, Capitol City Texas)

Of course he would have liked to break the story. In the first twenty years of his career he had broken more than his fair share. He too knew the power of the pen. He also had his radio show, the website with message boards and frequent appearances on the State University network as well as on local sports television. Since he was unable to break the story, he would deliver the biggest impact.

There are two ways to pick a fight in Texas: the first is to politely ask someone to step outside before punches are thrown; the second is to just walk up and sucker punch somebody. The Blogger-Radio Host chose the latter. The Baptist University was starting to feel attacked by the media, and the Blogger-Radio Host was about to bring the attack front and center by punching the Baptist University in the proverbial mouth.

The Blogger-Radio Host wrote a letter to the Baptist University President. The letter questioned how the President and the head of Judicial Affairs handled the internal investigation of the Transfer Player. His questions were detailed, to the point. He challenged the President's political past and connections. He questioned how, despite his experience, the awful manner in which he had addressed the alleged sexual assault. He took the attack on the Baptist University to a new level. He made it personal by accusing the President of mishandling the assault.

The Blogger-Radio Host sent the letter to the Baptist University President. Then he posted the letter on his website. He read and talked about the letter on all his shows. The main point question he raised was this: how could it take the Baptist University so long to come to a conclusion of a sexual assault that was completely opposite of that concluded by a Grand Jury?

Little did the Blogger-Radio Host know the Baptist University administration wanted to know precisely the same thing?

When someone is sucker punched, everyone watches to see what happens next. The Blogger-Radio Host, like The Writer, also enjoyed reading his readers' comments. It was the very first comment that got his attention: "Why is this story only being covered by in-state rival media? How come the national media isn't more involved?

The Blogger-Radio Host smiled like the Cheshire cat and thought to himself, "You just gave me a wonderful idea!"

The Reporter
(Early September 2015, New England)

When she arrived at her office, there was a rather large overnight package on her desk. The Reporter knew it was safe to open because she recognized the label. It was from her friend, the Blogger-Radio Host in Capitol City, Texas.

They were friends. They were not in contact on a regular basis, maybe a couple brief phone calls a year. They'd check in, compare weather, and make vague plans to get together. They'd worked together in the sports department at the major newspaper in Big D over ten years ago. Her current boss, the head of the Investigative Department for the Network, had worked with both of them there as well.

After opening the package and throwing away the bubble wrap, the Reporter pulled out stacks of paper, which included trial transcripts, copies of trial evidence and piles of related newspaper articles. There was a note at the top from the Blogger-Radio Host. It read, "You will need more, but this will get you started!" There was also a copy of an old bumper sticker from the 1980s, which read, "Don't Mess with Texas." She immediately picked up her phone and called her friend.

After exchanging "Hello" and "How are you," she asked "So… what is all this? Why did you send it to me?'

The Blogger-Radio Host replied, "Your next BIG story, babe. You need to cover it. It's totally in your strike zone. Every aspect of it falls into your well of expertise, I promise."

The package was timely. Ever since her "criminal activity of college athletes" article a couple of the schools were putting up resistance releasing the requested information. She was involved in litigation against two of the schools. And she was personally suing the schools - along with the Network. One of the legal battles she was winning. A university in Michigan was fighting to appeal a lower court's decision forcing the release of the records.

The one she wanted, her crown jewel, was the legal battle with Catholic University. She was currently filing an appeal to try to overturn a lower court's ruling not to release the records. The chances of collecting the information from the Catholic University were dwindling. She was prepared to take it to the state supreme court if necessary.

The package she received from the Blogger-Radio Host was like a birthday present. If she was unable to obtain the coveted information from the Catholic University, she would continue her quest by pursuing the largest Protestant university in the country.

She was about to blurt out, "Thank you God," but instead she found herself wondering, "How does this feel?"

"Excuse me?" said the Blogger- Radio Host thinking the Reporter was talking to him.

"This is so great, and timely!" she told her friend. He had read her criminal activity article but he did not fully understand her comment. The Reporter continued talking as she sifted and glanced through the contents of the box. "I have been looking for a school where I could investigate deeper criminal activity among the student athletes especially if the activity is sexual assault. Wow! Thank you."

"By the way," the Blogger-Radio Host said, "the Texas Senate just passed a law that subjects private universities to respond to FOIA requests. This should make it easier for you to get the information you need. I had an attorney friend get the information. The names of the victims and witnesses are in there. Go get 'em. Check out the message boards when you can. The fans at the other conference schools hate the Baptist University, and they hate the coach. The comments are naaaasty!"

"I will when I have the time," she responded. " I can't thank you enough. Why'd you reach out to me?"

"Come on. I trusted you when we worked together. I trust you now. You're the perfect mouthpiece and advocate for this issue, you know that. Besides, I hate those Baptist University bastards. The sooner they go back to irrelevancy, the better it is for us. The better it is for the State University football team, the better it is for me. We'll want to get the momentum going on this thing." And then he changed his tone, "So how soon before you can put an episode on air?"

The reporter answered, "Oh, gosh," calculating in her head, "This fall? End of the year at the latest."

"Oh, okay. As a just reminder, I'm friends with guys who cover the State University team and the conference. We get together for drinks regularly. I also have a former player who follows over 1300 related Twitter accounts. He is king of social media; he blasts and retweets. All four of us are ready to help," said the Blogger-Radio Host.

"Thanks again," the Reporter said.

"Remember me when you win your award!" the Blogger-Radio Host said with a smile in his voice. His subscribers loved hearing "bad news" happening to conference rivals and he looked forward to the articles the Reporter would write.

"I will. Bye," she said as she closed her office door and shut off her cell phone. She had work to do and could not be bothered.

She had already prepared the FOIA requests before she called her boss. She had two hundred seventy-five names of Baptist University football players on the FOIA letter, as she marched to the office of the Investigative unit department head. She told him she wanted the story.

The Department Head said, "Here's the thing: The Network is covering the story with the Network's own beat writer in Capitol City and one of the Network Columnist. They were there when the verdict was announced at the trial of the Transfer Player. The beat writer's only a hundred miles away from Central, Texas. They're on it."

The Reporter was relentless, "No, *I'm* on it. It needs to be my story. It needs a woman's perspective. I rarely go over your head, but I am committed to this. If you're saying no, I want the Network Executive to decide. If he says no, I'll stand down."

The meeting with the Network Executive lasted longer than expected. He was intrigued enough that he had his secretary cancel his next appointment. He said, '"Now, Tell me again your plan one more time?"

The reporter said, "I have the names of the victims and witnesses from the Baptist University trials. I want to run a piece through our investigative unit, so I can expose the Coach and the University. He turned that program around in his third year there. I have a theory on how he did it and I want to prove my theory."

Tapping his pen on a pad of paper, the Network Executive made a decision. "Done," he said.

"The network beat writer needs to be off the story," the reporter said. It was more of a pleasant demand than a request.

"Done. Can you work with the columnist? I want to have two people covering the story just in case additional resources are needed," stated the Network Executive.

"Yes. Be happy to have a team. I want to interview and film the victim and the witnesses. I also plan to film the Defensive Player who is in jail. We are going to show how the Baptist University did not properly address the prevention of sexual assaults and how they failed to help the victims after they were assaulted.

"Done," he said again.

"I doubt it will be necessary, but what if we need to pay the women for their stories?" she asked.

"Whatever you need, you have my full support, the Network Executive confirmed.

She and the Department Head left the executive's office together. When they were out of view from the Network Executive, the Department Head fist bumped the Reporter. "Wow that was a first. I have never seen him so responsive."

Back in his office, the Network Executive-with the ragtime melody in his head-sent a text to the Booster. The text read, "Happy days are here again!"

The Coach
(Late October 2015, Central Texas)

Number two in the nation. A part of him expected it. The other part of him could not believe it. He knew and felt the pressure that a college football team would have to have six to eight consecutive years of success to be considered a national powerhouse. Winning the conference was great. The bar had been elevated. A National Championship was in sight. This was year three. He was determined that the Baptist University football team would not be a flash in the pan.

The team continued to persevere. The starting quarterback broke his neck, but the freshman back-up stepped in and kept the offensive machine going. With every setback on the field, his team was able to step up and overcome. On the field the Coach could not be more proud of his team.

Off the field, however, the season was off to a rough start. The Baptist University had hired a new Title IX Coordinator. Even though the school's Judicial Affairs department had functioned in that capacity, the university was following new federal guidelines. What made it confusing was that the university was exempt from certain Title IX statutes because of its religious affiliation to the Baptist denomination and had difficulty determining which ones applied. The uncertainty hampered the administration's ability to adequately communicate to other university departments.

The Title IX Coordinator was investigating a 2013 case. The victim had refused to press charges. Here, two years later, the Coach still needed someone to detail how the new system and Title IX process worked. He was unaware of the incident from two years ago. Once it was brought to his attention, however, the player was dismissed from the team. The next semester, he would end up expelled.

Another off-field incident involved a former offensive coordinator and a current member of the Baptist University coaching staff. The former offensive coordinator was now the head coach of another program in a different state. The staff member went to visit the former offensive coordinator but he visited on a day that his current team was playing one of the Baptist University team's conference rivals. This visit was an NCAA infraction and the Baptist University head coach had to file the incident with the NCAA and apologize.

The Baptist University had hired an outside law firm to investigate all the issues relating to Title IX. The firm had concerns about how the athletic department handled situations where they were aware of sexual assaults. The Coach thought his position was clear: Any victim should be encouraged to press charges. "I'll handle the discipline of either suspension or dismissal from the team once charges were pressed," he told himself and others. That was his role. Discipline would not delay pending a legal outcome. He knew from experience and from other head coaches that if charges were not pressed, the player would automatically tell any coach that the sex was consensual or that it was just "play time." Regardless, he told his entire coaching staff to fully cooperate with the investigating firm.

The Commissioner
(October 2015, Big D, Texas)

The Commissioner was good at maintaining control. He knew how to make his point while maintaining order. Immediately after the conference meeting, he pulled the Baptist University President aside and wanted to know why the university had two players (the Defensive Player and the Transfer Player) convicted of sexual assault in a period of a year and a half. The Commissioner was pleased to find that an east coast law firm had been hired. He appreciated the proactive measures being taken by the President. It showed him the President was taking the situation seriously. The Commissioner offered no support; he simply made it clear that he wanted to be kept informed of the results and did not want to get his information from the media.

The Reporter
(October 2015, New England)

The key was getting the victim to agree to do the televised segment. The Reporter explained that during the interview, the victim would have a pseudonym and that her face would be shadowed. It was critical to get her on board so the Network could then approach the other witnesses to be a part of the airing.

The Reporter was surprised how quickly the victim agreed. Any rape trial is emotionally taxing on the victim, who had to relive the events of her publicly. The results of rape kits and SANE exams can be embarrassing in front of strangers. The Reporter knew from experience that a fast "yes" and quick agreement was always a good sign. It meant that the victim wanted some form of retribution for the pain she experienced.

Once the victim agreed, two of the witnesses agreed to be a part of the show. Only one witnesses from the trial had no interest. The Reporter was going to offer money, but decided not to pursue the third witness. It did not really matter because the third witness was never a student at the Baptist University anyway.

The segment was not about uncovering the truth, nor was not about showing inconsistencies in witness stories or testimonies. Those responsibilities had belonged to the DA and the defense attorney two years previous. The Reporter story's was to exploit an institution's failure to protect its female students, assaulted by members of its football team. The Reporter wanted to show that the girls were victimized for the sake of winning football games.

The story was bulletproof. Answers to several of the questions were spoon fed during the interviews. Like any segment, there were a number of re-takes to make sure answers contained certain information needed to emphasize the Reporter's storyline. She could use the girls' quotes verbatim. Their stories were embellished well beyond their respective two year old testimonies. In a courtroom, what the girls were saying would be considered "hearsay" and thrown out as inadmissible. But this was no trial, subject to the rules of evidence. They could say what they wanted so long as it whispered of truth. The words were golden to flesh out the storyline.

Her biggest frustration during the process was the time wasted visiting the Defensive Player in jail. ""What an idiot," she expressed to the Department Head. "Did he really think I was there to get his side of the story?" She was hoping he would tell her what the Coach or the administration knew of his alleged assaults. He was not helpful. He would not talk about his case. She allowed him to make a few statements about how football players are put on a pedestal and targeted – that was all she needed. The filming of an inmate would positively impact her storyline. The public assumes guilt when a convict appears in prison uniform.

Ironically, the two female witnesses were spectacular. They came across on video better than the victim. It was their emotions and their stories that made the segment so compelling and credible. Of course, the Reporter knew the backgrounds of the witnesses. She knew exactly why the DA used the two girls for witnesses instead of pursuing additional counts of sexual assault. Both witnesses had had consensual sex with the Defensive Player, in addition to their assault incidents. This fact of consensual sex would confuse a jury. When the girls included the names of the Coach and names of administration as part of their interviews, the Reporter thought to herself, "Yes, make it personal."

The victim was a tougher subject. Since the victim was never a football fan or a Baptist University football fan, her statements that the school cared only about winning games were unconvincing. Perhaps because she was gay, she seemed "hard". The Reporter was disappointed in the girl because it was her assault that started this downward spiral for the Baptist University, and the Reporter knew that public sympathy would not be as strong as it could be. In the end, however, the Reporter knew it would all work out great for the victim.

During one of the breaks from videotaping, "Are you going to file a Title IX legal claim about the university?" the Reporter asked the victim.

The Reporter explained that universities are mandated by the government to help victims of sexual assaults.

"Seriously?" the victim asked. She had no idea.

"Yes", said the Reporter. "The Baptist University did not have a Title IX Coordinator at the time of your assault and it appears that they did an insufficient job of trying to keep you in school. You may want to consult an attorney. Victims are awarded a lot of money. Some of the settlements have been $800,000 or $900,000."

"You've got to be kidding!" said the victim as she contemplated the possibility of that kind of money.

The Reporter told her, "You may want to act fast. Time is of the essence. Each state has a statute of limitations to respond."

"What does that mean?" asked the girl.

"You only have so long to file a lawsuit from the date of your sexual assault. In Texas, its two years; four years under special circumstances." The Reporter knew this fact from having lived in Texas for so long.

"Thank you so much," said the victim. She was thinking that receiving cash for her hardship was more than a silver lining.

"Do me a favor. If you decide to file a lawsuit, please let me know right away?" The Reporter gave her a card with her cell number and personal email. "However, I can help." said the Reporter.

And help she did. The Reporter made sure that the editing department deleted certain quotes that the victim had remained at the university for a year after her assault and that she received free counseling.

The Coach
(December 2015, Central Texas)

The season wound up with major disappointments. The Baptist University team lost not only the starting quarterback but eventually the back-up quarterback to season-ending injuries. The Coach had to convert a third string quarterback to wide receiver earlier in the season, and then convert him back to quarterback even though the player had not taken a single snap as quarterback in practice. The player did not hold the QB position very long; he suffered a concussion during the second-to-last game of the season. The game still went into double overtime, but the Baptist University team lost.

What happened after that game was a shock to the Coach. They were playing the Private University in a cold, heavy rain. Obviously, the Private University fans and students knew how the Baptist University Coach felt about having to share the title of Co-Champions the year before with them. As the Private University student fans rushed on to the field, the Coach expected to hear name calling. When he heard "Rape Monger," he was not really surprised. When some of the Private University fans got close and spit at him, however, he could not believe that the level of hatred had risen to such an extent. He expected disrespect; it comes with the territory of being a college coach. But the intense vitriol caught him off-guard.

The last game of the season was against the State University at home. The Coach had no quarterbacks, so his fourth wide receiver played a wildcat version of quarterback. During the game, the kid threw an interception and made a hard tackle on the State University defensive back who intercepted the ball. A couple of the State University players came off the bench and the sideline and pushed and jumped on the newly converted quarterback. When his team cleared the bench to run across the field to join the brawl, the Coach made no effort to stop them. The players defending one another were a sign of team unity.

The Coach was a straight shooter. He called things as he saw them. He made his post-game comments about the fight. He did not care if they were considered insulting to the State University team. He loved his players; he was loyal to them and to Baptist University. The Coach wanted to reinforce his loyalty to Baptist Nation by claiming he represented only Baptist University. Once, when his star receiver complained that his hamstring was feeling tight, the Coach advised him to sit out the upcoming bowl game. The player argued that the team needed him, especially since it did not have a quarterback. The Coach did not want the player to risk getting hurt, thereby hampering his chances of going high in the upcoming draft. He assured the player that the team would be fine, and that he needed to take care of his family, and a draft in the first round was the best thing for him. The Coach preached team first, but sometimes a player's family was the player's "A Team."

There were more important things in life than winning football games.

Network Executive & the Reporter
(December 2015, New England)

"What do you mean you are not going to air the show?" The Reporter gasped. She could feel blood pulsing in her temples as she sat across from the desk of the Network Executive.

"I didn't say we won't air it; what I said was that we are not airing it this year," he said coolly.

"It's broadcast ready. Editing is finished. Every week that passes, the momentum wanes," the Reporter stated, trying to stay calm. She would lose credibility if she became too emotional.

"Not necessarily. I want to air the segment, and know when the time is right," said the Network Executive.

"Ok, then when?" snorted the Reporter.

"It will air February 2, 2016." You can put the web version online on the Network's site the weekend before. Don't ask me why. I have my reasons," the Network Executive said.

"Fine!" The Reporter fumed as she marched off to her office. She did not want the Network Executive to see the frustration she was feeling inside.

The Network Executive had his reasons. February Third was national signing day. He wanted to see how the Coach would handle the hot seat of a nationally broadcasted segment. The Network Executive was curious to see if any of the Baptist University recruits would remain loyal and stay committed to Baptist University.

Same time, the Reporter's office

The Reporter sent a quick text to the victim. It read, "Story will go out end of January. You did great!"

The victim texted back, "Thanks. FYI I hired an attorney. He said really good case. You were right."

"Smart decision. You did the right thing," the Reporter replied. She was proud that victim had pursued her suggestion.

"We may name the Coach in the lawsuit. What do you think?" the victim texted.

"Strategic," the Reporter sent back. The Reporter did not have anything personally against the Coach. His Texas accent and roots were too much personality for her. She knew her associates enjoyed interviewing him and speaking with him.

Fact: He was the head of the football team.

Fact: He was part of the University.

Fact: The University was the problem.

Fact: The more personal the fight gets, the better the media coverage.

Fact: She was leading the media coverage.

The Coach
(February 2016, Central Texas)

He knew there would be a segment about the school on the Network. There was no sense being anxious about its airing. The campus and the town saw the Network's cameramen and trucks. When the season came to an end, and the Network had not broadcast a show, the Coach optimistically thought the University might have dodged a bullet.

It was not a bullet that was fired; it was a bomb that was dropped. What was exploding was the Coach's cell phone. He purposely did not watch the segment. He knew that if he did, his reaction would be highly emotional and that he would be unable to argue or adequately defend the segment's base storyline. He also did not watch the show so when he was asked by media sources, he could truthfully say he had not watched it. The Coach had enough family members and friends who told him everything that was in the segment. Their renditions of it made him sick to his stomach.

The calls and the texts that came in from the Class of 2016 recruits and their families required all of his attention. He had to tactfully control the damage. His responses included.

"Yes, the team will be OK."

"Yes, your son will still have his scholarship."

"Yes the whole recruiting class is staying intact."

"No, we are not going anywhere."

"No, there are no NCAA infractions or investigations."

The recruiting class was loaded with talent. It was considered the best in the conference. That some of the kids were being contacted by other coaches made his blood simmer. "What low-life snakes," he thought to himself as he sat in his office responding to the inquiries until his cell phone ran out of battery life.

As he was walking to his truck to get the cell phone charger, the Coach was bothered by how the Network portrayed the unresponsiveness of Judicial Affairs and the Athletic Department to the sexual assaults. The Network completely disregarded the due process that had been taken. The segment made it seem that the University did nothing, once it was informed of the incidents. One of the alleged assaults occurred three years ago and the girl was coming forward now, even though she had had consensual sex with the Defensive Player before he was even at Baptist University. The other girl did not immediately notify the school when her alleged assault took place. But those who watched the segment told the Coach the show made it seem as if the school buried the information. Even though the athletic department's relationship with Judicial Affairs was not very good, the Coach was sure that no one he knew at the University just "sat on" information.

Kicking a rock across the parking lot with his cowboy boot, the Coach was still uncertain how he as the head coach was expected to do something when no charges were pressed or especially if the police were still conducting open investigations? Was he supposed to assume a player was guilty until proven innocent? The segment made the university look foolish. The Network believed the school should have doled out punishment at the first words of the victim; even Title IX cases require statements from all parties to be examined.

He regretted not having said a few words in a Network interview. But then again, his Administration would not allow him to comment at the time.

The Reporter
(March 30, 2016 New England)

Sitting in her office, the Reporter's cell phone vibrated with a new text. This was the text she had been waiting. "We are filing today, flying into Texas tomorrow for news conference. Thank U"

The Reporter texted back, "Nervous?" She used the grimacing emoji for emphasis.

The victim responded, "A little. All good. Trial was way worse." She followed by using the sad face emoji.

The Reporter texted back, "I bet."

One more text came back from the victim, "We are adding the coach to the suit."

The Reporter fist pumped the air. While she did not have anything personally against the Coach, naming the Coach meant her story could continue while a lawsuit was pending. Now the Network would be covering the lawsuit which would mean it would continue for at least a year, unless a settlement popped out of nowhere.

Logging on to her Twitter account, the Reporter text back, "I am going to tweet it out now. It will help your cause. My followers will love hearing the news."

There was a couple minute's delay before the next text arrived.

"I am using my name," the victim wrote.

The Reporter was puzzled. She was unsure if the victim was saying what she meant to say. Was she filing the lawsuit using her real name instead of Jane Doe? This is truly taking the attack to an elevated personal level. Victims rarely use their personal names. The Reporter was guessing her attorney needed the "personalization effect" added to give it greater merit and credence.

The Reporter began tapping the keys on her laptop's keyboard. She typed in the victim's name, announcing the lawsuit against the Baptist University. She deleted it just in case she misunderstood the victim's intent of using her own name. She typed, "Rape victim to file Title IX suit against the Baptist University." She checked Twitter to make sure she was the first one to tweet it. The victim had told her that she would be the first to know.

"Wait, what?" the Reporter said aloud. She discovered her tweet was not the first. It was second. The first tweet announcing the lawsuit was sent a couple hours earlier. It was sent by a staff writer at the local paper in Central Texas. Her initial feeling of being betrayed immediately diminished. Of course they should know, she reminded herself. The local newspaper was holding the press conference. It was okay. She could live with second place.

As she closed her laptop, she thought to herself. "Personally named plaintiff versus personally named defendant."   These were the things she loved about her job the most. The story had just begun.

The Coach
(Late March 2016, Central Texas)

The Coach received the news as he was driving home. He pulled into a convenience store/gas station outside of town, he needed to think. Sued?! Lawsuit?! "Negligence, for what?" He had not driven the victim or the Defensive Player to the party. He did not buy any booze for them, or serve them drinks. He did not own the apartment complex. How is he supposed to control the conduct of every one of his players, let alone the women that want to hang out with them? How is anyone supposed to control the conduct of other adults? His mind was racing, and not one of his questions had answers.

Why was he held responsible to report to Judicial Affairs? Judicial Affairs already had all the information. They had the information before he did. Bottom line: there had been too long of a gap in time without a Title IX coordinator in place. That's where the University had exposed itself, but no one was admitting it. He noticed his knuckles were pale white from gripping the steering wheel so tightly.

Taking a deep breath, he called the Baptist University President and felt a little better after the call. The President explained that the University carried Errors &

Omissions liability insurance for these things. The insurance carrier would instruct them what to do. Attorneys would be assigned to represent the school and the coach. They had plenty of time to respond to the petition. The Coach was told not to worry.

Big talk from the Baptist University president was okay. The Coach needed more reassurance, so he called an attorney friend from his hometown. Stepping out of truck to get another deep breath of Texas spring air, his attorney friend informed the Coach that to date only two other head coaches had been named in Title IX lawsuits: a football coach and a basketball coach from two different Pacific Northwest Universities. One of the cases was dropped; the other was settled quickly. Neither of them came close to going to trial.

The attorney explained that under Title IX regulations, an individual cannot be sued personally, since individuals do not receive compensation directly from the federal government. He further explained that the lawsuit most likely would be thrown out since it was beyond the Texas statute of limitations. He encouraged him to relax. The insurance carrier for the Errors and Omissions would manage the process.

Although the Coach felt better after the conversation, deep down, he was still anxious. It was the first Title IX lawsuit the University would face (many other lawsuits would soon follow). He did not like being named in a lawsuit. All of the legal jargon was unfamiliar territory for him. As he mentally tried to prepare for the lawsuit, he felt like a fish out of water.

The Visit
(April 2016, Race Car City, Indiana)

A small group of men from Baptist University exited a private plane that left Big D, Texas that morning. The group was comprised of members of its governing board and administration. There was little conversation amongst the group; each face wore a serious expression. A waiting courier van was to take them to a very important meeting. The meeting could determine the ultimate fate of the Baptist University football team and other team sports. The meeting was with the NCAA.

The purpose of the meeting was to let the NCAA know that the Baptist University had things under control. The group brought up the possibility that a few other law suits may follow. The findings from the law firm would be presented sometime in the next month or two. Based on the findings, if the group determined that NCAA infractions had occurred, they would offer self-imposed sanctions on the football team and coaching staff. It was a long, but necessary trip for such a brief meeting.

When the men boarded the plane to return to Texas, their mood was definitely lightened. It was the right strategy to be proactive with the NCAA. It was important to show the NCAA that a plan was in place. A few of the men silently enjoyed a cocktail, while a couple others let their seats recline and closed their eyes to nap; another just stared at the peaceful clouds out his window. The humming of the plane's engine had a calming effect on the group. But it would be the last calm before a fierce storm was about to devastate the university.

The Regents
(April 2016, Central Texas)

The Baptist University was governed by a Board of Regents. The board was an overseeing board that met four times a year. They were not involved in the university's day-to-day operations, and were not regularly present on campus. The operations were to be performed by the administration. The Regents were simply overseers.

The Board consisted of approximately thirty individuals. They were business owners, high level company executives, attorneys, and a few pastors. Almost every member of the board was an alum or had children who were students attending the university. All of them had "deep pockets." It was an honor to serve as regent - a status symbol.

The most influential committees on which to serve were the Governance and Student Affairs committees. The Finance committee was important when borrowing was necessary. Right now, the university did not have any capital projects in the works. The stadium was the last major project and it had been completed two years ago.

The chairs of the Governance and Student Affairs committee were lawyers. It was designed that way in case they were needed to offer "unofficial" legal opinions. These two men along with the board president were part of the executive committee.

When the school commissioned an outside law firm to investigate how sexual assaults were handled at the Baptist University, the two attorneys were assigned the point persons for obvious reasons. When boards choose attorneys to be the lead on special projects, risk assessment and cost analysis criteria are replaced by legal protection procedure.

Back in the fall of 2015 when the law firm was originally commissioned, two proposals were made. The difference between the proposals involved the depth of the research. The more expensive option offered forensic tracking of computers, emails and phones. One of the Regents asked, "How are you able to access the data from smart phones? Is it hacking?" The answer came back, "Not when the phone is issued by the university or cell data goes through the university cell towers." The attorney Regents knew how valuable discovery information could be; it was their recommendation to choose the more expensive option.

In the end, the law firm was hired for three reasons. First: to determine why the outcome of the trial and the University's internal investigation of the Transfer Player was different. Second: to set up systems and processes to ensure that the entire university was Title IX compliant. Third: to determine what were the athletic department processes for handling off the field problems when they arose with players?

The two attorney Regents, along with the board president, would be traveling east to meet with the law firm to hear their presentation of findings. Preliminary information already signaled that there would be concerns with the athletic department. They still had to file an answer to the lawsuit allegations. The three Regents drafted a list of concerns the board would be facing in the near future.

The list read:

1) Will the errors and omission policy cover us and pay for our legal representation?
2) More lawsuits would follow for incidents that took place in 2011-2014.
3) Would the NCAA launch an investigation?
4) How should the school communicate findings and information to parents and alumni?
5) How should the school communicate to the current student body?
6) What action would the Commissioner and the conference take?
7) Would the university lose financial support from some of their big donors?
8) Who is going to take responsibility for this mess?
9) What will happen to the Coach?

Three sets of eyes all looked at one another after items 8 and 9 were written. No one said a word, but ironically each reached the same conclusion individually. With a silent nod, they knew what they would have to recommend.

The Reporter
(April 2016, New England)

She was surprised the Network Executive called her directly. Over the last four months, he'd been very curious about when the next article would be finished. He wanted to know how much more information the Reporter had, and how much longer it would be for her to continue reporting on the sexual assault situation at the Baptist University. He wanted her to present the information often, as if she'd just discovered new information. Even though she received the FOIA requested information all at once, he wanted her to stretch it out to make the story last longer. In every article, she always highlighted how the University was obligated under Title IX requirements, and how long it took the university to install a coordinator during that period.

Because of her relationship with the victim, she was able to schedule other reporters and divisions of the Network to interview her. Once, the Network was in such a rush to get an interview aired, the Network spelled the victim's name incorrectly as a subtitle. A box of Network logo athletic gear was sent to the victim with a personal apology from the Network Executive. The victim was ecstatic to receive the items.

The Network covered extensively any news about the Baptist University. Early that April, the Reporter ran an in-depth article about two more football players who were possibly involved in another sexual assault. She had obtained a police report in which a victim clearly did not want to press charges because she said she was not sexually assaulted. There was a two year gap from the time when the police report was written and the time that a Title IX investigation was performed. The police report was from the municipal police department. The report claimed that the Baptist University was made aware of the incident.

When the Reporter questioned the chief of police, he had no idea who the reporting officer would have contacted at the university. He stated that they are under no obligation to contact the university. If there is an ongoing investigation, the chief of police did not want any meddling from anybody outside of his municipal police department.

It was not important to the Reporter who at the university was contacted. What was important was that when she interviewed the victim, the victim said no one from the university had contacted her at the time. Since it was in the report it had to be true, except the part of the victim stating that she had not been sexually assaulted. The Reporter used her experience and cleverness to decide which facts and information each storyline needed to contain; no way would she credit her insightful journalism as a God-given gift. No, she acquired the expertise through her hard work and her devotion to her career. She was the journalistic authority on sexual assaults and the other criminal acts of collegiate student athletes.

A new story fell in her lap and the timing was perfect. One of the Baptist University's elite defensive players had been arrested for sexual assault. The player had graduated in December and was waiting to be drafted. This new story shed light on the fact that Baptist University sexual assaults were not just past problems.

The Network Executive was interested in keeping the Coach front and center with each report because of his company's exorbitant investment in the State University's network. Any mark on Baptist University, would strengthen State University's position, and his bottom line. The Reporter had to be careful not to write anything that could be considered slander. The Reporter did not have a personal axe to grind with the Coach. But he did work for the Baptist University, which stood for everything she was against. She hated its perceived hypocrisy. With every article, she got a little more satisfaction that she was somehow besmirching the good Lord above.

She certainly had much to share at the upcoming Investigative Reporting Exposition where she was slotted to be a keynote speaker. The events of this story came easy, almost too easy. There was so much information to digest. Things just seemed to place. She looked forward to what would happen over the next several months.

The Regents
(Mid-May 2016, Central Texas)

The next meeting with the east coast law firm was devastating. Many of the men were shocked to learn what had transpired at the school they were overseeing. They had been too caught up in the hype of all the good that was happening at the University. Ranked football teams, beautiful new stadium, giving was at the highest, enrollment increasing; it was such a great time to be a part of Baptist Nation. Until now.

They were the overseers. How were they to know about Title IX? None of them had even heard of the "Dear Colleague letter" the federal government had sent out to the university. They were businessmen, attorneys, pastors. The president of the university was a former judge. How in the world did he miss this important requirement? Every university is required to report sexual assault in its annual security report. Their university even reported sexual assaults. Why did no one bring it to their attention, even those assaults that were listed in the reports? What were they going to do?

Besides the rich Baptist heritage, the university had a history of how it handled lawsuits. Over the past seventy years, when lawsuits against the university started to become prevalent, the Baptist University's mode of operation had been to separate itself from the offending party. If a fraternity held an off-campus party and something happened at the party, it would be the responsibility of the fraternity. If the university thought there would be the threat of a lawsuit, the infracting group (fraternity) would be kicked off campus, even before any facts were presented to the administration. The problem now was that the head of the administration and leader of the athletic department were involved. What would they do?

Because the Board was named as a defendant in the lawsuit, their meetings were more frequent. Most of the Regents would gather in a large meeting room in the administration building. A few others would conference in to the meeting via telephone. Nervously, one regent stood up and suggested that ultimately the Board of Regents was responsible and that they should bear the consequences. Right or wrong, what happened at the university occurred on their watch. He reminded them that there are sins of omission as well as commission.

His motion was dramatically disregarded. Other Regents argued that they could not admit culpability. If they did, they would not be protected by the Errors and Omissions insurance policy; plus they had images and reputations to maintain. The regretful regent made a brief argument about integrity, but it fell on the deaf ears of the rest of the board, who strongly believed they had zero responsibility in the mess.

Many people would be affected by their decisions. One decision was simple, and the vote unanimous: the university president would have to step down. He was extremely popular, and while there had been no Title IX coordinator, there was broad knowledge of the sexual assault awareness programs he had put in place. But those programs did not outweigh the absence of a Title IX office. It was his ultimate responsibility for the school to be in governmental compliance. He failed in that duty.

He would be removed as president, but he would remain on staff at the law school. He and the Coach had become friends, and there was evidence that the Coach leveraged the relationship to keep a player in school when the player was on academic probation. Demoting the president was the easiest.

The more difficult situation regarded the fate of the head coach. In regards to sexual assaults allegedly committed by members of the football team, there was no concrete evidence that the Coach knew or withheld any information that the Judicial Affairs office did not already know. There was no evidence that he personally and purposely interacted with any victim to convince her not to report or press charges. There was a body of evidence showing that once someone pressed charges, the Coach enacted the appropriate discipline.

The law firm had uncovered texts, which revealed certain situations where the Coach did not want to report some of the off-the-field incidents to Judicial

Affairs. These incidents involved marijuana usage, brandishing guns, and players exposing themselves. These were the issues that became gray areas for the Regents. If the Coach knew about these, would inferences be drawn that he might have known about the sexual assaults too? No one had clear answers. There was no evidence that could support any inference of the coach's knowledge of sexual assault.

The E&O insurance policy clearly stated the carrier was excluded from providing coverage if there was any "deliberate fraudulent or dishonest act or willful violation of statute, rule or law committed." The lawsuit was filed in federal court since it was a Title IX case involving sexual assault. Although The Coach would not be connected to any involvement of campus sexual assaults, there was damning evidence that the Coach had not wanted to report some of his players' minor infractions to the administration.

The Coach's contract provided a clause that unless there was just cause, the coach could not be fired. Once again, he did not give his players marijuana. He did not give any players weapons that they might show in public, and he certainly would not send a player to a masseuse and tell him to drop his towel. The Regents found the decision making complex, it was difficult to know exactly how much of a player's behavior was the coach responsible. The Regents were feeling the weight of the decision.

If they fired the coach, seven years left on his current contract would need to be addressed. They would have to pay him or buy him out, or engineer some kind of financial settlement. The best recruiting class in the conference would leave. Other current players could opt out and take a year off and transfer to other schools. The current coaching staff would be disgruntled and impact the team negatively going forward. The Coach was endeared by the school's largest donors. They would not want the Coach to be fired and leave. Together, they all had built the finest football venue in the country. Baptist Nation had achieved so much in a relatively short time.

One regent suggested that they all stand together and wait for the entire legal process to pan out. They could keep everything intact. They would tell the media that they do not currently have due cause and should the situation change, they would make the appropriate adjustments to discipline. It was a sound and logical plan that made sense on all fronts, until a letter from the conference Commissioner was read at one of its meetings.

The Commissioner's letter called for two things. He wanted to know how the University was going to respond to the lawsuit. And the letter demanded to know the results of the law firm's investigation. The Commissioner wanted to see the issue resolved quickly. He did not want the problem at the Baptist University to be construed as a conference problem. This situation should not reflect poorly on the conference; otherwise the Baptist University was going to have new and bigger problems to resolve.

A new strategy was put in place - a brilliant plan. The Coach would be suspended for one year, with the intent to fire, and then reinstated. The suspension would continue to show willingness of the Regents to punish the university leaders. The suspension would show the NCAA that the university was proactive in handling its own sanctions. The suspension would demonstrate that the Regents were exhibiting institutional control in a terrible situation.

The coaching staff would remain intact. The recruited players would stay knowing that the beloved coach was coming back. The big donors could live with a one year suspension. The Regents would be buying time, maybe a year or more for the lawsuit to pan out. Eventually, the stories would die down and the lawsuit and the two trials would be yesterday's news. The insurance carrier stipulations should be satisfied. The vote and the support for the plan should have been unanimous.

There was a small faction, however, that insisted that the Coach be brought before the Regents. They wanted to see what responsibility Coach was willing to take. They wanted to know what lessons the Coach had learned, and what he would change in the future. They wanted to make the Coach pay for putting them in this situation. They were embarrassed. Failure to install a Title IX office as mandated by the federal government was truly inexcusable. The lawsuit and sexual assaults were all their friends wanted to talk about at parties, church, and the country club. They were pestered by "little verbal digs" from their friends and family who were alumni from other schools in the conference. This faction was getting sick of having to address the negative attention. They needed the "spotlight" to be on someone else.

While the meeting that evening may have had the appearance that the board was united, it was not. Any chain is only as strong as its weakest link. The small faction had a mole. The mole leaked the strategic plan to the press.

The Reporter
(Mid- May 2016, New England)

The information she had received from the Blogger – Radio Host and the information from the FOIA requests was starting to dry up. She was able to put together another article to keep fuel on the fire. Once again, the power of hearsay works great in print even if it's not court testimony under oath. The Network Executive gave her clear marching orders to keep referencing the coach, coaching staff, and athletic department.

The leaked information about the Coach possibly being fired was reported in a Texas newspaper so she was able to quote them as a source without risking a libel suit. The Network Executive loved that she suggested that the Coach may be fired. By reporting it, the national media could support the proposition of a termination. Ultimately, it was the Coach's responsibility wasn't it? It was a great momentum builder.

 She was able to point out that players were not disciplined after the coaching staff had been informed. She was able to add reports of physical assaults. Since the victim's names were in the police report, she was able to call and interview the victims. The girls were willing to offer information on their own. The Reporter did not have to pay for any of the stories.

One incident involved a girl going to the football team chaplain to report a physical assault. The girl thought for sure the chaplain would talk to the Coach and the President. She assumed that conversations among school authorities on her situation had taken place. But if she assumed conversations that were supposed to have taken place did; she also must assume that no disciplinary actions were enforced. It was easy for the girl to say her ex-boyfriend football player was never punished, whether true or not. And if the girl said it, it was even easier for the Reporter to quote her.

In another case, The Reporter was able to reach a former football player and his alleged girlfriend/victim from five years previous. She discovered the incident in a separate police report with a different football player. Both the former player and the girlfriend were willing to talk with the Reporter and both stated there was no sexual assault. The girl was not a student and had also been involved with other football players. But, because it seemed there were ongoing issues between the girl and the former player, the municipal police department kept the file open. If it was an open police file, the municipal police could not make the information public. If the municipal police department was unwilling to share information, it could be inferred that they were hiding information. And if they were hiding information, they must be protecting someone. The Reporter was very good at creating the storyline she wanted her audience to understand.   She could make anyone believe everything she had written. She was so remarkable at presenting information, her readers were able to draw connections and make inferences of events that *might* have transpired. It was no surprise that she received national media accolades and awards, and no wonder she was always asked to be the keynote speaker at investigative reporting industry meetings. Persistence and in depth investigating was her strong suit.

She certainly did not see any attempts by God to try to prevent her stories from being told and printed. Maybe more proof that He did not exist or that that he approved. If God existed, the "Great Almighty" could surely prevent her from reporting. Regardless, there was satisfaction in having the Baptist University under media scrutiny. Her reporting was justice for the victims as well as their hurt and pain. Retribution felt good, and feeling good was rewarding.

The Coach
(Late May 2016, Central Texas)

Similar to a kid being sent to the principal's office, it is never good to have to go before the entire Board of Regents. The Coach had learned a long time ago not to show emotion. It was not because he thought it was a sign of weakness, he just never wanted anyone to feel sorry for him. It is why he never made excuses in his personal life or for his football team.

He knew there would be a roomful of angry eyes on him. He knew the question in everyone's mind would be how could this happen on his watch? It was the same question he asked himself every night before he drifted off to sleep and then at least twice during the night as he awoke during fitful sleep. It was the same question he asked when he was unable to finish his biscuits and gravy at breakfast. What could he have done differently?

The pressure to win for a college coach is intense. You are paid to win games. In the absence of conference titles, many are fired. The Coach continually put pressure on himself to be better each year. He wanted to be the best team in the country. He loved his players, his coaching staff, the friends he had developed and he loved Baptist Nation. He stood up for fans everywhere when no one else would. Not only was he loyal to the Baptist University, he was unapologetic about that loyalty to the media.

The feeling of loss was overwhelming and saddening. A feeling that he had known all too well as a younger man, had come crashing back on him now. He was saddened at the possibility that his players had harmed others. He was sad that he might not be able to finish building a nationally recognized powerhouse football program. So many people involved; so many lives impacted. The weight of it all was almost unbearable.

The Coach wore a coat and tie for the meeting. No one waited with him – alone he paced up and down the hallway as he waited to be called in. The knot in his tie felt extra tight against his dry throat. He could feel the perspiration roll down his back. After what seemed like a game with five quarters, he was called in. As the Coach stood in front of the Regents, he was asked what he would do to change things going forward.

The Coach took responsibility for setting up a system in which he was the last to know. He admitted that he had made some mistakes. Then, despite everything in him, he broke down and cried.

There were no dry eyes in the room. The Coach told the Board that he would do as they wished. He would accept their plan. They were all in agreement with a plan except for a few who wanted to see his head on a platter.

The Blogger Radio-Host
(May 2016, Capitol City, Texas)

He loved having "the scoop" and his subscribers paid good money for his. And inside information from a disgruntled person was always the best. He may not have broken the story about the sexual assault trials, but he definitely broke the story about the Baptist University severing their relationship with their president and the head coach. Now that he knew there was a strategy in play to possibly bring the Coach back in a year, he would do everything he could to ensure "the intent to fire" resulted in more than intent. The subscribers loved hearing good news about the State University football team, but they thrived on hearing bad news about all conference rivals.

For the last four unrelenting months, he and his his "team" at the multinational news agency, largest sport's magazine and social media wiz had successfully attacked the head coach and the Baptist University football team. When the news was announced that the Baptist University coach was suspended with the intent to fire, a tweet was sent out from the social media wiz to the "team" members, the Reporter and the Department Head. The tweet read, referring to the media team – "They did their job. The victims are whom we should be thanking." The Blogger thought the tweet was too bold and wished the "team" recipients hadn't been personally named. Everyone on the "team" had recognizable twitter accounts except the social media wiz. Thousands of tweets go out every minute; this tweet would soon fall back into everyone's twitter account history. It would all but disappear. The Blogger-Radio Host knew the social media wiz was untraceable.

The Coach

(Late May 2016, Central Texas)

The Coach cared about his players like family. He invested as much time as he could into their lives. He loved interacting with them on the practice field and in the weight room. The Regents had made it clear that he was not to call a team meeting to announce he was no longer the head coach. He was numb from the shock of losing his position; the Coach did not push back and argue about not being able to have a personal meeting with his players.

He paced back and forth on his deck before sitting down in the rocking chair. He was so filled with emotion he wiped the tears from his eyes using the sleeve of his long-sleeved athletic shirt. He sent a text to all his current and former players how difficult it was to report that he was no longer going to be the head coach. He appreciated their love, trust and loyalty. He encouraged them to stay motivated and faithful. He told them he loved them.

He was overwhelmed again in his life with feelings of loss. Tears that come from mourning are tears that help the healing process begin. These tears were because his heart was broken.

The Writer
(May 2016, Capitol City Texas)

The Writer was anticipating the best way to launch her book. It was scheduled to be released later that summer. In her book, she had exposed the playbook that college athletic departments deploy when one of their players gets accused of sexual assault. It was a great read and well written. She was contemplating how to get more attention and increased book sales. She was twirling a pencil through her fingers like a rock band drummer thinking about new ways she could market the book.

Her phone rang. It was her Software Developer friend, and he sounded wired and upset. "What's wrong?" she asked.

"The Baptist University fired its coach," her friend replied.

"I know! It's great news," she replied laying the pencil down.

"Not if it gets traced back to me. Our Director of Nursing friend is worried too. He regrets the pedophile comments," the Software Developer said. There was urgency in his tone.

"No one is going to ask me anything. In the event they do, we will say you're a source and I don't have to reveal your identity. It is like you are my priest." she snickered at her own joke, picturing her friend wearing a clerical collar.

"I closed my account. I haven't posted anything under that account for months," he claimed. He was worried someone would try to find him.

"You are worrying about nothing. You are fine. Enjoy this moment. The Baptist University will soon be back to being irrelevant. Ding, dong the witch is dead!," the Writer said as she pictured the Coach's feet sticking out of Baptist University stadium. Her image had him wearing running shoes, not red sequined boots.

She was unsettled that her friend was so shaken by seemingly nothing. Perhaps in the IT world, anonymity is simply a myth.

The Regents
(Late May 2016, Central Texas)

Now that Regents had separated ways with its president, fired the Assistant Coach and another staffer on the football team, and had publicly announced that the intention was to fire the head coach, they had the difficult task of deciding how they were going to make public the findings from the law firm. The conference had already demanded to know the conclusions from the investigation. The Regents were cautious to accept anything in writing from the law firm because they were concerned that others would subpoena the information.

Based on the presentation they received from the law firm, they drafted a thirteen page "Finding of Facts," and made it public. It would serve as a template to implement all the changes that would make the university Title IX compliant. Current employees, former employees and current and former students were interviewed. The students were identified as being victims and survivors of assault (physical and sexual).

The university was front and center with the media because of the sexual assaults. The document clearly stated that the administration, on occasion, deterred complainants from reporting or pursuing student conduct processes. The football program was accused of failing to identify the sexual behavior of one of its players and failing to respond when it found out about possible sexual assaults. The conclusion was that the football program had a tone and culture. Players' were not held accountable for their conduct. Interestingly, not a single football player was interviewed during the process.

The conclusion was neither an oversight nor a mistake; it was designed to shift the blame and responsibility. The goal was to move the media spotlight away from the university and aim it on the Coach. The Commissioner's letter was clear- it was the Regents' responsibility to contain the problem. It was the Baptist University's problem. Do not let it spillover onto the conference.

The Commissioner
(Early June, 2016 Big D, Texas)

It was the second letter the Commissioner had to write in less than four weeks. He attempted subtlety. If he was blatant, it could raise red flags. He had private conversations with both of the state schools in the conference. They were elated. "Ecstatic" would be the proper term to describe the reaction to what was happening to the Baptist University. Goal #2 was being accomplished and he didn't have to do a thing.

Half-kidding to himself, he hoped the two state universities would not send a group of hookers to the Baptist University team in an attempt to put another nail in its coffin. He still wanted to know what the law firm had found. In part, he wanted to be prepared in the event the NCAA launched a major investigation. He also wanted to see if there was any tangible evidence against the Coach.

He rarely said he hated anyone. It was always bad politics to have that strong an opinion. Even if he hated somebody, he made sure it didn't show public. But he *hated* the Coach. Karma is a bitch, and what comes around goes around. The head coach would eat the words he had spoken to the Commissioner when he announced the co-championship in 2014. The Coach and the Baptist University had suffered from tunnel vision. He had zero sympathy for both; they had dug their own graves.

The letter stated that the Baptist University should make sure that the law firm's findings matched the University's decisions regarding its relationship with the Coach and the University President; the conference would have issues with the school if its disciplinary actions did not adequately align with its conclusions. If an NCAA investigation was launched, the conference would comply with the NCAA completely. The Commissioner wondered if now the Coach had wished he represented the conference as well as the Baptist University. He wanted the school to assign three Regents to keep him abreast of the pertinent information because the Baptist University President had been dismissed from the university and there would be a void at the conference meetings.

The two state universities wanted the Coach gone. They were sick of sharing the conference title and sick of losing top recruits to the Baptist University. They were right. Cut off the head of this monster and the body will die. If the Coach goes, the football program will die. The Baptist University did not have the long history and national recognition that the two state schools had. The Baptist school had its turn, and now the two state universities had determined the ride was over.

The letter was clear. He would hold them to their "intent to fire." If the Regents started to get serious about trying to bring the Coach back in a year, the Commissioner would get tougher. He was not going to write a letter that stated "Fire the jackass; that is an order." The Regents should know how to demonstrate "institutional control."

The Advocate –
(June 2016, Pacific Northwest)

Timing. Sometimes the effects of unrelated events in different places and over time can converse later - the Advocate had a story. It was her story of a gruesome, despicable sexual assault that happened to her when she was a young woman. Every father and mother should have their daughter hear her story as a warning and a caution about what can happen at a college party. Her story was picked up by the collegiate division of the largest sports magazine in the country, which asked her to write an op-ed piece and give an opinion about what had transpired at Baptist University.

She kept up with the recent developments at the Baptist University. She read the thirteen-page Finding of Facts that brought back the memory of her own horrific sexual assault as well as the intense feelings of betrayal and hatred. Because the Coach was named personally in the law suit, she assumed the events of what happened at the Baptist University were the same ones that had happened to her years before.

Eighteen years ago, she was a twenty-four year old single mother at the time living in a Pacific Northwest college town. She was not a college student. She was dating a football player at a university in the Pacific

Northwest at the time. She and a friend had gone to the apartment of some football players to hang out and have drinks. There were four men in the apartment; two were football players for the university. One was a football player at local junior college and the other of whom was a football recruit.

Although toxicology reports did not show evidence of chemicals, she said she was drugged because she was unable to control herself and prevent the assault. The four men all took turns with her sexually. She was humiliated still more because she was violated with even a flashlight. In the morning she described herself feeling like "a piece of garbage". She had dried vomit in her hair. She had a used condom stuck to her stomach and she was wrapped in a sheet of filth.

She decided to press charges. The University was aware of the assault and the head coach was aware of what his players had done. They were suspended for one game and had to do community service until a verdict was reached at the trials. The players' lives were disrupted for one game - basically four hours. Her life was destroyed.

The District Attorney explained that each of her attackers would have to be tried separately. He told her that she would have to tell her story four different times in front of four different juries. She was told it would be a difficult case because there was no evidence that she had been drugged and she had willingly gone to the apartment and consumed alcohol. One of the attackers was in high school. The trials would absorb a lot of her time.

Extra time away from her sons would be a problem for her, so she decided to drop the charges. For the next sixteen years, she lived a tormented life. She frequently contemplated suicide. She was so angered that the university did not discipline the men. When she read some of the quotes that the coach had said about his players, she hated him more than she hated her attackers. He described them as good boys who made a bad decision. Every time she recalled those words, she fumed all over again.

After eighteen painful years, she, with the help of a sports writer, reconciled with the Pacific University. In three weeks, she was about to reconcile with the head coach from Pacific University at that time who was now coaching at a different university in the Midwest.

What happened at the Baptist University struck a nerve. She would be a voice for sexual assault victims everywhere. She would speak to football teams and share her story with the hope of preventing other terrible sexual assaults across the country.

While she was going to use her time and story for a greater cause, she was painfully unaware that she was also about to be used for someone else's agenda. The agenda: the complete removal of the Baptist University's Head Coach.

The Coach
(Mid-June, 2016 Central Texas)

Once again, the Coach went for a drive in his truck to sort things in his mind. If the plan was to bring him back in a year, no one bothered to tell him and no one made sure the entire Board of Regents was in agreement with the plan. It is like calling a play in the huddle but not telling the quarterback which play. The Coach found out from a donor friend, someone who had connections with many of the current Regents. The Coach thought the meeting with the Regents had gone well and he naively believed that they would all be able to work together and make the appropriate changes. They would learn from the past and be a better institution going forward.

He turned off the AC and rolled his window down to feel the hot Texas air blow across his face. Apparently, the Regents thought differently. They decided to suspend the coach with the intent to fire; he had not expected the intent to fire. At worst, he expected some form of suspension, but not termination. He needed clarification and more information. What would he say to his coaching staff, his players, his wife and family? Why did the media already know about a plan to bring him back in a year as head coach?

171

His thoughts turned in on him. The media was focused on his firing, and was relentless about it. The Coach wanted to see the evidence against him. If they had any justifiable cause, they could force him out of his contract. He still had eight years left, worth nearly forty million dollars of income. On the contrary, if there was no evidence, then he would be wrongly terminated. The Coach was convinced that the information the law firm had would show that he did nothing wrong.

As he approached a four way stop going in a small Texas country town, he realized he was over an hour from home. The sixty miles had escaped his conscious thoughts completely. The Coach strategized that if the Baptist University was wrong to terminate him, he would have to file a claim against the school. But he didn't know how he could file a claim against the school and work against the school's attorney - the same attorney representing him in the victim suit against him. The Coach determined that another meeting with the Regents was necessary to settle everything. He was in pile of shit, and it was getting bigger every day. His shovel was getting smaller.

The Commissioner
(Mid-June, 2016 Big D, Texas)

The Commissioner prided himself on level headedness. He had designated three Regents to be his points of contact. He was not going to wait for one of them to call him and tell him the results of the second meeting with the Coach. He was going to be proactive this time- to say the least.

He called one of the Regents from his office. After exchanging brief pleasantries, he directed the Regent: "Call me after the meeting is over; I want to know the final decision before tomorrow's news."

The Regent begrudgingly replied, "I will."

The Commissioner continued, "Did the law firm find incrementing evidence that showed the Coach had prior knowledge of anything, or interfered with any victims who wanted to go to your Judicial Affairs?"

The Regent replied, "No, not in the area of sexual assaults, otherwise we would have terminated his contract out-right."

The Commissioners stated boldly, "Right now he is bad for us, and bad for the conference. I know you are without a president but my expectation is that you get a

Lane Alpert

handle on everything." He had no questions; he was just making a statement.

The Regent replied, "Commissioner? He is very popular and adored by many. When it was suggested that he be brought back after a suspension, I thought leaking the strategy was the wisest move. Pressure to have him completely gone is going to have to be from outside. He is endeared by almost every one affiliated with our school."

The Commissioner was not going to offer support or help in any way. "The conference won't tolerate this controversy in the spotlight. Get your issues resolved and get them resolved quickly. What is your plan?"

The Regent responded, "We're going to buy out his contract. He gets more than a fair sum and we'll pay it out in installments. A gag order will be in place and the Coach will have to be silent. It'll be as if he has ten pairs of socks down his throat. He will be unable to say any disparaging words. Any questions for the Coach or requests for interviews, relating to the university or the lawsuit, will have to be cleared by us."

The Commissioner said, "I was surprised what transpired in the media last time; I don't want any more surprises."

The Regent added, "One more thing: We have an interim head coach in place." He hoped that the appointment would be a welcomed ovation to the Commissioner.

The Commissioner ignored the comment, "Just make it happen. This circus needs to end. The conference is losing patience."

"Understood," the Regent responded humbly. He was eager to have this conversation over. The Commissioner unsettled him and the additional scrutiny didn't help.

The Commissioner wondered whether the Regent really did get it.

The Coach
(Mid-June 2016, Central Texas)

Time and the pain of loss had impaired his ability to recollect most of his childhood memories. Standing on his deck, staring into the distance, he remembered years before the conversation he had had with his mom about doing the right thing. He recalled her standing in their kitchen, wearing her apron and holding a wooden spoon, instructing him on the importance of doing the right thing.

Naturally, the life time of pain avoidance meant that he still struggled with doing the right thing. And there were so many people involved now it was unclear what doing the right thing really meant. He questioned whether signing the financial settlement with the Baptist University was best: he thought of his family and providing for them. He thought of the football players and the coaching staff, especially his good friend, the Assistant Coach, who had been fired. He thought of the high school players he was currently recruiting. Even though the division between the Baptist University and the Coach was widening, he thought about the friends that who were Regents past and present. He thought about the unfilled requests for the evidence of his alleged involvement in the sexual assaults by the football players. He thought about the control he gave the Baptist University over his life by signing the settlement up to and including preventing him from even meeting the victim. Could an apology that addressed the hurt the victim experienced with the Defensive Player even help? How does one apologize for something he didn't do? This was difficult; the Baptist University had told the victim and her attorney that the Coach would meet with them but once again no one told him about a meeting. The Baptist University had to maintain control. Some of the Regents were ruled by fear; the Coach's honesty could prevail in his answers to questions, and they could not risk the consequences.

Did he make the right decision by signing? Did he do the right thing? Taking off his cap, he scratched the back of his head. "Life is hard," he whispered to himself.

The quietness of the moment left him melancholy. He knew so many people. He had been so popular a year ago. Everyone had wanted his attention, his time or an autograph. As he stared out at the Texas country, he had never felt so alone. The wind that blew through Central Texas, even on that hot summer day, sent a chill down his spine.

The Advocate
(Mid-July 2016, Central Texas)

She was not sure whether the invitation to speak to the Baptist University football team was initially meant to be a publicity stunt. She had just publically slammed the Baptist University and the Coach in a national blog posting. She was committed to her mission of stopping sexual assaults on college campuses. She had a message to present; the players needed to hear her story, and besides the Baptist University was a paying customer.

One month ago, she had reconciled with the former Pacific Northwest University coach who *only* gave her attackers a one game suspension. That coach and the interim coach at the Baptist University were friends with one another. Both men though it would be beneficial to have the Advocate speak to the Baptist University football team.

She was pleasantly surprised at how kind the interim coach was towards her. He had taken her to dinner the night before and was sincere in the questions he asked. She had expected a hostile environment because of the article she had written, but the players were welcoming and respectful. She was impressed that change was not only possible, but welcomed.

The biggest surprise was the media attention she received. Every major sports media outlet wanted to talk to her about her experience at the Baptist University. The free publicity was great. Her public speaking bookings were unparalleled. Although she knew her personal story would have a strong impact on college campuses, she did not know the impact would be so swift.

The Commissioner
(Late July 2016, Big D, Texas)

The conference was having its media days. Before the Commissioner would address the media, however, he met confidentially with nine of the ten conference presidents to specifically address concerns and a course of action that the conference would consider in addressing the sexual assaults at the Baptist University. Missing, of course, was the Baptist University President. What was said behind closed doors in the hotel executive suite that day would not be repeated outside the room.

The Commissioner wore his power suit, conservative tie and a heavily starched white cotton shirt and sat at the head of the table. He looked like a United States Senator. He looked at each of the nine faces staring back at him. The Commissioner could accurately guess what each one was thinking. He knew the Baptist University did not have a single advocate in the room. If it did, he knew that person would not have the testicular fortitude to speak up. Several of the schools wanted a "pound of flesh" from the Baptist University. Their attitude reminded him of a chapter from the book, *"Lord of the Flies"* when the boys wanted to sacrifice the fat kid. One of presidents asked - pleased with himself- whether the conference had legal grounds to go after the Baptist University.

The Commissioner had already looked into the matter and coolly replied that they did not have any legal recourse. He wondered if any of these men, some of whom had their doctorates, had taken the time to read their own university's annual security reports. Had they done so, they would have found that all nine other schools each had more sexual assaults than the Baptist University.

The Commissioner's goal was not to amplify the problem, but contain it. Keep the focus on the Baptist University; don't allow it to spill over onto the conference. Overflow would be horrendous and could jeopardize his job. The option of kicking the Baptist University completely out of the conference was raised. But a decision that drastic would surely involve litigation and he asked the presidents to be patient to consider any ramifications. He reviewed the conference by-laws with the presidents and reminded them that, any major discipline would require a supermajority vote. It meant eight of the nine schools would have to support the decision.

The "make them pay" motion started to gain momentum around the table. The Commissioner stood up and educated the presidents. Seventy-eight% of all sexual assaults involves drugs and alcohol; Seventy-three% of all college sexual assaults happen to freshman and sophomores. He stressed to the men that because there were underage kids breaking the law, publically it would be wise to hold the Baptist University accountable for the events that occurred. But as a conference, the more important motivation should be to eradicate sexual assaults at every conference school.

The presidents could see the wisdom behind the Commissioner's recommendations. He assured them he would do everything in his power to get the Baptist University issues resolved. The national media was focusing more on the Baptist University football team than the school. The heart and soul of the football team was its coach. The Network was leading the charge against them. Before they opened the doors, all ten men were in agreement and were confident that the Commissioner would maintain the pressure and contain the problem to the Baptist University. To contain it meant decisions about the destiny of the Coach would be necessary. The Commissioner and the presidents ended the meeting, but not before consensus that this problem would go no further than Baptist University.

The Commissioner left gleefully, and headed straight to the swarming media. There he thought the biggest topic of public conversation was going to be a conference championship game and expansion. He was prepared for those questions. But over half the questions were related to sexual assault at the Baptist University. For this he was ill-prepared.

New lawsuits against the university had been filed since his last talk with the Regents. The gag order on coach was in place. A severance package had been accepted. Why would the media not move past the sexual assaults?

He was an expert at reading audiences. He had a knack for knowing follow-up questions before they were asked. The Commissioner fixated on the Blogger – Radio Host's nods and glances. He also observed the writer from the largest sports magazine and the reporter from the multinational news agency exchanged knowing glances after each of their questions.

It appeared they had the same sixth sense that he did: the head coach might return to the Baptist University. They had their own separate plan to prevent his return. Despite this present shift storm, the Commissioner could tell they had an agenda, but he did not need any help now; plus, the entire matter was embarrassing for the conference. The Commissioner made no further announcements that day. There was no sense bringing more attention to this looming crisis. Though he didn't know it then, a different set of warning bells was about to be rung.

The Commissioner
(NEXT DAY: Late July 2016, Big D, Texas)

The Commissioner enjoyed his morning run. It kept him fit and gave him a chance to clear his mind before heading to the office. He was in such disbelief when he read the morning paper; he hoped that when he screamed expletives that he didn't wake up his wife. He went to the Google App on his phone to see if the online articles were reflecting the same sentiments as the newspaper. There were already two screens of Google hits in response to his search.

The Commissioner had made a point in the Q&A yesterday to point out how unified the conference was on eradicating sexual assaults from all of its campuses. Using the knowledge about sexual assault statistics he had shared with the conference presidents, he addressed the public about the challenges of eliminating sexual assault when drinking and hormones were prevalent. The media took the comment completely out of context, and lambasted the Commissioner for making it.

The stress immediately negated the post-run euphoria he had experienced moments before. There was no way he was going to fight the media. There was no way he was going to let this happen to him again. Not in his wildest dreams did he never think his remarks would be taken so out of context and twisted in way that made it seem that he was supporting the Baptist University. In fact, the exact opposite was true.

After removing his workout clothes and jumping into the shower, he let the cold water run down his body, washing away the tension he had experienced after reading the article. He would learn from this event. Whatever amount of pressure he felt he had needed to apply to the Baptist University yesterday, was going to have to double from here on. He would call the executive committee of the conference, which consisted of the State University, the Other State University, and the Great Plains University. They would implement the plan they had previously agreed – go public that the conference was demanding additional information from the Baptist University and requiring compliance with conference demands. He would individually call the other conference presidents and encourage them to be thinking of other types of discipline that could be applied to the Baptist University if no one sensed that enough improvement had been made by October- the next conference meeting.

If the media was going to attack for his comment, the Commissioner could only imagine what the media would do to the Coach; not that he cared. He recalled the gag order on the Coach, and so he called one of the Regents to remind him and the Board the importance of the Coach not speaking in public. If the Coach went public, containing the problem would be impossible.

The Network Executive
(July 2016, New England)

He rarely drank alone, or before 5:00 PM. And his usual go-to was Laphroaig neat. Today called for something special. The Booster had given him a bottle of premium vodka distilled in Capitol City, so he poured himself a double. Special occasions usually call for a toast and this was one of those occasions. The nemesis Coach had been fired, and he could not defend himself, either because of the litigation or the contract buyout. The recruits were leaving. The State University picked up three of the four-star recruits along with others who had departed from the Baptist University.

The boys in Capitol City did a masterful job in the media trenches keeping stories alive and attacking the Coach, the University and the football team. The Reporter was masterful and the Network Executive had already decided she would get a raise for the story coverage. The Commissioner was seething, however, and was ready for it all to be over. He had the Regents' proverbial testicles in his hand and he was prepared to squeeze and twist. The Network Executive made a note to himself to send a Christmas present to the national sports magazine writer who brought the Advocate into the mix. The Advocate was a godsend to his cause. He always said it is better to be lucky than good.

One toast now, another when he was sure the Coach would never return, and a final when the Baptist University football team had a losing season.   He pulled up a picture of the Coach on his computer screen; he hung up his suit jacket on the back of his office door as he closed it, and rolled up the sleeves of his business shirt.   He touched the edge of his computer with his drink.

"A man may kiss his wife goodbye.

The rose may kiss a butterfly.

The beer may kiss the frosted glass.

And you, the coach, may kiss my ass".

The Vodka was very smooth.   And recent events made it all the more enjoyable.

The Coach
(September 2016, Central Texas)

Trying to get the Coach not to say something was like trying to leave a puppy in a room full of leather and telling it not to chew. As more lawsuits were filed against the University, the allegations piled up. It seemed the media was having a field day after each filing. They would find the most outlandish allegation or piece of hearsay quote and use it as a headline.

The Coach wanted to apologize but his hands were tied. He couldn't say anything of the players who were convicted, nor address any criticism because of the lawsuit. He couldn't even say that the lawsuit was refiled removing the Title IX claim against him personally, a bogus tort allegation just to keep him on the claim.

He wondered if he should have refused to settle with the university. Then, he would be free to speak about everything. But things moved so fast, and he was so numb at the time, that he agreed to settle to care for his family. What is done is done. He could not undo it.

He called the Network and set up an interview. He wouldn't subject himself to the Reporter, however; so he contacted someone whom he knew would be impartial and objective, since he had some things he needed to get off his chest.

He left the cap and the long sleeved sports attire at home in the closet and he donned his coat and tie. When the cameras started filming he admitted his shortcomings, apologized and took responsibility as the head of the football team. He was sorry for the pain that the victims experienced. He admitted mistakes and vowed to do better.

When it was over, he was relieved. He felt better. He hoped the world knew he was sorry for what happened and that his apology would be accepted. He wanted to move forward with his life.

A couple weeks later, the Baptist University football team was scheduled to play the Texas Harvard University. The Coach debated whether he should attend. On one hand, he wanted to show support to his team, but he knew he could not address them directly in the locker room or on the sideline. Since his settlement, he knew he would never be invited to speak at a practice or game. The Baptist University football game was being played in Humid City, Texas. The Coach went to the game to support his players and staff. He sat where the fans sit. He did not wear the colors or logo sportswear of the Baptist University. It killed him not to be on the field. But when the Texas Harvard marching band formed the letters "Title IX", he was reminded by the pain that accompanies loss. It was all a huge slap in the face to his team and the Baptist University.

The media spotted him in the stands. They immediately sent reporters to where he was sitting to try to get a comment from him. Some of the media outlets even accused him of coaching from the fan section. They were trying to allude to the notion that he was sending in plays or signals to the coaching staff. The Coach soon realized that from here forward, nothing he did would be taken at face value. The media would accuse him of a personal agenda and ulterior motives. He realized he had made a mistake by attending. He had only wanted to show his support. The separation between him and his team was growing. And with each separation increased, the hurt returned.

The Network Executive
(September 2016, New England)

It was the first email he opened that morning. The Network Executive could not believe the Coach wanted to apologize. Texans don't apologize. The word "sorry" is not in their vocabularies. The Network Executive did have some concerns that if the Coach appeared sincere and remorseful, it could potentially stop the negative publicity wave crashing down on the Coach and the Baptist University.

The Network Executive insisted that the Reporter handle the interview. He could trust her to ask the hard questions relentlessly. The Network Executive knew the Reporter was already prepared with questions should the opportunity rise. When the Coach's attorney refused to allow the Reporter to be a part of the interview, the Network Executive begrudgingly agreed to have a different network employee conduct it. He did not want the Coach doing the interview with another station or network. Internally, the Network Executive made it clear that he wanted to see the final edit before it was aired. He sent the Reporter an email requesting that she attend the editing meeting for the piece. He wanted the Reporter to insure it would not deter from the master storyline she had delivered.

The interview was over an hour long. The segment was only thirty-nine seconds. The list of follow-up questions was given to the Network's anchors and its affiliates with the instructions "Do not deviate from the provided questions." The anchors asked the interviewer if the Coach was sincere. Did he know why he was apologizing? What was his demeanor? In the end, the piece made the Coach appear that he had "no clue" why he was apologizing. Damage had been contained by the network – the Coach was still determined to be a "bad guy." The Network Executive was pleased.

The Network Executive had become an expert at anticipating potential confrontations that might arise. The Network Executive knew the Booster might want to have a say about the segment. In preparation for that conversation, the Network Executive purposely had someone place a State University football helmet in the background of the segment when the network interviewer was being questioned about the interview with the Coach. The Booster would see the State University logo, and be less inclined to want to make changes (which provisions in the contract allowed him to do) to the aired statement.

The Reporter
(September 2016, New England)

The Reporter was constantly receiving accolades from the Network Executive about her work and the storyline she had reported over the last nine months. Co-workers were constantly stopping her in the halls to give her feedback that the Network was so pleased and deemed her as one of the most valuable employees it had. She was honored that she had been their top choice to conduct the interview with the Coach, even though it ultimately had to be a co-worker who conducted the interview. Up until this year, she did not have much direct correspondence with the Network Executive; most of the communication came directly through her boss, the Investigative Department Head. But now, it had become commonplace to receive phone calls or texts directly from the Network Executive.

Her phone chimed letting her know she received a text. The text read, "Coach's apology is BS. Need your help." It was from the Network Executive.

She replied , "I am wrapping up an article now. Be ready later today." She had just finished a Network's article for the on-line edition.

An immediate text came back, "Good news on article. Need you to contact victim. Check your email. "

The Reporter opened her email which had an attachment. The attachment was the transcripts from the Coach's interview. The Network Executive wanted the Reporter to set up a video feed so they could get a televised response from the victim. He said The Writer in Capitol City had already agreed to be on the show. The Network Executive gave the Reporter the assignment of sharing with the victim's attorney, the comments from the Coach. And, this was not a request; it was a demand.

The Reporter immediately shot a text to the victim. "Coach was on TV. Need your response on coach apology. Sent copy to your attorney". The victim was always quick to reply.

The victim replied by text, "Ok. I'm calling him now. Thank U." The reporter had also sent some available times.

The challenge for the Reporter was the short amount of time the victim would have to prepare for her response. The Network Executive was chomping at the bit to have the response immediately. The Reporter knew the victim was a poor subject on video. Ever since the first showing almost a year ago, the victim still came across as unconvincing. She could not portray herself in a way that the general public would sympathize with her. Her answers were flighty and nonchalant. It was frustrating for the Reporter, so she sent along with the interview transcripts, a list of questions that would be asked. Hopefully, her attorney would prepare the victim for the presentation style of answering the questions.

The victim texted back, "We will be ready. I'll be at attorney's office for video feed." The victim and her attorney changed their schedules to accommodate. Getting air time on the Network was a great means of supporting her case.

The purpose of airing the response was to counter-attack the Coach and make his apology seem insincere. Of course, the response did not include the fact that the Coach's apology was restricted because of the settlement with the university and the pending lawsuit. The Network did what it could to display insincerity and insensitivity from the Coach.

Apparently, the airing of the response was good enough for the Network Executive. The Network was prepared and ready to go toe to toe with responses and comments from the Coach or any of his supporters. After the airing, The Reporter, once again, received thanks and more accolades from the Network Executive.

The Commissioner
(September 2016, Big D, Texas)

The Commissioner knew the Regents would screw it up; they were so emotionally torn in so many directions, and incapable of making the mess go away. Everyone knew more lawsuits were to follow. The lack of a Title IX coordinator for so long, made the school susceptible of legal action in the event that any alleged sexual assault happened during that time period. But the Commissioner was infuriated when he saw an interview with the former Baptist University President that took place during a festival in Capitol City, of all places.

The Commissioner watched on-line snippets of the video interview. He read and re-read articles and quotes that were written about it. The former president claimed that the Coach had been wrongly criticized, and was an honorable man trying to improve the lives of the young men he coached.

The Commissioner's mind was racing. A needed mid-day run was completely out of the question. He leaned forward at his desk, rubbing the temples of his head with hands. He kept asking himself the questions, "Why would the former president support the Coach?" Why would he do it only a couple weeks after the Coach's so-called apology?" "The former president had hired the law firm to conduct the investigation; why was he now contradicting the findings?" Of course, he asked only himself these questions in silence of his office. They were rhetorical. Whether the former president made the statements because he felt guilty for his part in the Coach's firing or did so because the Coach asked the former president to speak on his behalf, he could not know. Regardless, the Commissioner saw the supportive comments as an attack on his mission and the conference agenda. Reading between the lines, he saw it as staging for the Coach to come back after the season hiatus.

The Commissioner could not find a pencil to snap at his desk, but two hard slams of his desk drawer relieved some of the frustration he was felt. Taking responsibility into his own hands, he was determined to end this charade. As long as the Coach was in the "public picture," the media circus - a thorn in the Commissioner's side – would continue. It had to end. The Coach had to be removed altogether; he must never return.

Because of the debacle at the conference media day where all the reporters just wanted to know about the events at the Baptist University, and the out of context quote the media held against him, the Commissioner set up a Sexual Assault Awareness Forum. A panel was chosen, a platform developed and the media could ask all the questions it wanted. If the media did not want to deal with the real facts involving causes of campus sexual assaults, they could confront someone else, but the Commissioner was not going to let it happen to him again.

 The Commissioner chose a famous professional running back who had been caught on tape assaulting his girlfriend, to be on the panel. He added a friend who was a university president in the conference (carefully not choosing a president from one of the state schools). The chief of police for Big D was included. He added the Reporter and the Advocate.   The Reporter, by then, had the Baptist University up against the ropes; the media would have a field day asking her questions. The Advocate was fueled by internal anger and he liked her boldness and that she had expressed harsh words about the Baptist University, as well as the Coach. He could not wait to see those two ladies in the same room. They had strong opinions about the sexual assaults and the Baptist University.

The Commissioner was pleased with himself for putting this together. No one would ever label him the architect of such frenzy. All he had to do was sit back and enjoy seeing Baptist University-one of his schools mind you – be eliminated as a competitor to State University or the Other State University.

The Advocate
(Late September 2016, Pacific Northwest)

After the forum, the two women met in the hotel bar. Sitting at an open booth ordering two glasses of Merlot, they began to share what they thought about the forum. The Advocate and the Reporter hit it off immediately: they had a mutual crusade to wage, and they became friends.

An incident had occurred after The Advocate's talk to the Baptist University football team this past summer, she relayed. The Advocate was going to initially let it go and keep her mouth shut about it. But she was not under any contractual agreement preventing her from sharing what happened in her presentations.

The Advocate told the Reporter that after the talk; one of the members of the coaching staff - an assistant coach - escorted her and the Title IX coordinator into his office. The assistant coach wanted to find out *the real reason* why the Advocate was there talking to the Baptist University athletes. Only one month before, she had boldly claimed in an internet blog that the school should get the death penalty from the NCAA. Her presence at the school did not make sense to the assistant coach.

He felt the Advocate was personally attacking his friend, the fired head coach. The assistant coach wanted the

Advocate to know that the Coach did nothing wrong. It was all a conspiracy against him.

She continued to tell the Reporter that the encounter with the assistant coach prevented the Advocate from interacting with the team after her talk. She reported the interaction with a Baptist University associate athletic director, and was told they would look into it. The Title IX coordinator had nothing to say about the discussion.

The Reporter encouraged the Advocate to go public with the encounter. The nerve of anyone trying to defend the Coach was atrocious. The Reporter reminded the Advocate that she was the voice of so many silent victims. It was not a time to speak; it was a time to roar. The world needed to know how extensive the problem was at the Baptist University, and how evil these student athletes were.

Putting down her wine glass, the Reporter grabbed the Advocate's forearm and looked at her seriously. The Reporter told the Advocate there was the possibility that the Coach might return. And if he returned, what would happen to the sexual violence prevention program the school had undertaken. The Reporter applauded the Advocate for her courage this far, but that she needed to voice her views about college sexual assaults among student athletes more loudly and more frequently.

Nodding in agreement, the Advocate agreed. She would continue to be a voice by speaking out against the school, and especially the Coach. She considered giving them back the money they had paid for her talk. She concluded that the school would not have fired the Coach if they did not have evidence against him. Right? The assistant coach's behavior validated in her mind that claims against the head coach were true. Right? If the Coach was fired, it wasn't for no reason; he was part of the problem and the problem needed to be fixed.

So even though she had reconciled with the Pacific Northwest Coach, and liked him, all she had to do to find her anger was to recall how he had implied her attackers were good guys who made bad decisions. She could hate again. Plus, she had started to receive some confrontational tweets on her twitter account from Baptist University fans. Some of the comments were rude and mean; others were threats. She could make a way back to a realization that, somehow the Coach was a big part of a big problem.

Yes, the Advocate confirmed she had to be a mouthpiece. The Reporter assured her that except for a few Baptist idiots on social media, no one would challenge the words of a brave rape victim survivor. Her story was her megaphone. They promised each other they would stay in contact.

The Advocate posted the story about the encounter with the Baptist University assistant coach on her blog.

She proclaimed that the Coach should never coach again – anywhere. The blog went viral.

The Coach
(Mid-October, Dog Pound City, Ohio)

He loved his home state of Texas, but fumed a breath of fresh air when he stepped off the plane. He had been asked to be a guest coach for a professional football team. It was a fun and healthy distraction; he was given and wore clothes bearing the logo and colors of the professional team. He walked past a locker room mirror and took a double take to see how he looked. The stress of his situation was evident. He needed to gain a couple of pounds.

He was briefly reunited with four of his former players from Baptist University. The professional football team wanted to tap into his brilliant offensive mind. And, it was refreshing for the Coach to focus only on football plays. He loved helping the professional team come up with ways to run up the scoreboard. He took a deep breath and smelled the freshly cut grass. For a brief moment, he relaxed and relished being back in his element.

But the moment was short lived. Once the media found out that the Coach was at the professional team's practice, there was a public outcry. The head professional coach was criticized for bringing the Coach to a practice. The pro coach defended the invitation as a chance to learn and improve his own team's offense. The media put so much pressure and so much attention on the pro coach and his team that the Coach's invite was cut short. It was an awkward and embarrassing moment when the professional team said good-bye. But the Coach understood the decision.

The plane ride back to Texas was two hours of mental torment. Legally and contractually, he was unable to defend himself against accusations and it was becoming problematic for him. People were drawing wrong conclusions. The media were lodging damning, inaccurate statements by quoting people who knew nothing about the situation. And still, the Coach was unable to speak publicly. He got to the point where he couldn't watch or read any sports news. It was disheartening, and the pressure was taking its toll.

The Coach never pointed a finger or blamed anyone. If the university did not install the correct processes for reporting sexual assaults, how was he expected to follow something that did not exist? Who was going to inform him that the legal process no longer mattered? Unable to defend himself, there was a shift in the underlying story that the media was presenting. The storyline was that the Coach was responsible for promoting a culture of sexual violence at the Baptist University and the players could get away with breaking the law.

The Coach never asked anyone to fight his battles for him. No media outlet would give him any amount of air time anyway. Once, a woman who was a fan of the Coach drove around campus for two hours in her RV. She displayed a "Restore Coach!" banner on the side of her vehicle. But this show of support, only got a few blurbs of recognition in the media. The Coach still had some allies and friends who believed he had done nothing wrong. But they too were being silent. The coaching staff was not; it was preparing to go public with its support of the Coach.

One of the players from the 2016 recruiting class was removed from the team because of two possible involvements in Title IX incidents. He was never given a chance to clear his name. The interim coach suspended him but the Baptist University administration did not want him in the school, anyway. And, any player who was suspected to be involved in a sexual assault was just too much of a risk for the university to have as a student or a player. So the University advised the student to move on to another school or declare himself eligible for the draft. The interim coach made clear that it was the administration's decision and not his. The entire coaching staff- all hired by the Coach - tweeted out this fact. They were staging their own war against the administration and the Regents. They thought that they were showing loyalty to the Coach and were working to get him back. Instead it sealed his fate to never return to Baptist University. The Regents would flex their administrative muscles in response. And there was nothing the coaching staff could do about it.

The Network Executive
(October 2016, New England)

The Network Executive thought the Network was thorough in covering, reporting and delivering the news surrounding the Baptist University. It had kept the story front and center in the media for quite some time. He thought everyone involved would be pleased until he received a call from the Booster.

The Network Executive answered his phone at his desk and heard screaming on the other end of the line, "THEY ARE STILL F'ING WINNING!" The Booster was irate.

The Network Executive explained, "They have a weak non-conference schedule; those wins were expected and they have won the games against the lower teams in the conference. But they only have one win against a formidable opponent." He was trying to lay out the facts but the Booster wasn't listening.

"I don't care. These are kids with a no name-has been coaching staff. They should have cracked by now." The Booster was gradually calming down.

"The team will crack. It will fall. It just takes time. They are under an immense amount of pressure. They are getting hit from so many sides. The Advocate keeps pouring it on them," said the Network Executive. He was not worried. It was just a matter of time.

"Well, as long as there is hope those damned Baptist kids are not going to give up. We need to get rid of the hope and turn up the pressure," the Booster firmly stated.

"What do you suggest?" asked the Network Executive. He knew the Booster was not going to just wait for the natural process to work itself out. The Booster had to be involved and busy.

"Well, I'm going to give our State University president an earful. He is on the executive committee of the conference and has the Commissioner's ear. I am going to tell him to turn up the pressure. Then I will call the Commissioner myself. I suggest you do the same." The Network Executive had no doubt that the Booster would make the call to the Commissioner. For his part, the Network Executive would not be as bold and crass as The Booster had been to him. But he would call the Commissioner and voice concerns and ask questions. He knew the Commissioner was almost at his breaking point.

Water boils at 212 degrees Fahrenheit. Energy had to be added. The temperature needed to be turned up slightly. The team would crack. Something would happen and the spiral to irrelevancy would take place for the Baptist University football team. He would make the call tomorrow.

The Commissioner
(Mid-October 2016, Big D, Texas)

He slapped his desk with both palms. It was over. The final straw had broken him. He was finished with the circus that was happening in Central Texas. Now the Baptist University's Title IX coordinator had quit and planned on suing the school. Every time he thought the school hit bottom, the floor dropped two more stories. He called his "favorite" Regent. There were no pleasantries.

Factually he stated, "Next week is the conference meeting; you will make a final presentation. Every conference member will walk out of the meeting with a clear understanding. The Baptist University finally has a plan for each of the issues it faces. It keeps getting worse with you," said the Commissioner.

"These things take time. We thought all the suits were over. The exodus of the Title IX Coordinator came out of nowhere," the Regent started to say. He was immediately on the defensive.

The Commissioner responded, "You're out of time! Let me officially go on record as saying this: Members of the conference shall demonstrate conference control since you were unable to gain it at the institutional level. The conduct of the conference members shall be

committed to comply with the rules of the NCAA and
the conference. Each member will accept responsibility
for investigating known or alleged violations at its
institution and will take prompt and effective actions.
Do you understand?"

"Yes," said the Regent.

"Supermajority vote can force the withdrawal of one its
members, do you understand what that means?" The
Commissioner asked.

"Yes," said the Regent.

"A withdrawing member, no matter the cause, is
subject to pay the buyout amount. Do you understand
those ramifications?" The Commissioner said with his
voice elevating.

"Yes," said the Regent.

"The buyout amount is forty-six million dollars. Do you
understand the magnitude of the amount?" The
Commissioner scolded.

"Yes," said the Regent.

"Supermajority is seventy-five percent. Do you
understand?" the Commissioner nearly yelled.

"Yes," said the Regent.

"Mr. Regent? I have enough votes." And the
Commissioner hung up the phone.

The Regents
(Late October, 2016 Central Texas)

A letter was sent to Baptist Nation; most received it via email. The only sentence that every alumni, student, fan, booster and donor read was that the beloved coach of Baylor Nation was never coming back. The page had been turned. Even the biggest optimists relinquished their last hopes for his return.

The Regents hired a national public relations firm to release the information.

On a Friday, after business hours, multinational media outlets were contacted by three Regents. The bottom line was that nineteen football players had committed seventeen sexual assaults. They were showing that they understood the gravity of what had taken place. One of the incidents involving a female athlete highlighted that the Coach knew about an incident and did not report it to Judicial Affairs. He was on record as encouraging the victim and her coach to report the incident to the police. She hadn't.

It would be a month before announcing the hiring of a new football coach.

They knew the Coach would react to the release of the information. To what extent, they were unsure? That was the least of their worries, however. They were hoping the Commissioner and the rest of the conference would be satisfied. Could they hold back the conference fury? No need to call the Commissioner; he would read it in the headlines. He should be satisfied. There was zero chance that the Coach would ever return to Baptist Nation. Now, they were praying that the Commissioner would not call for a vote to kick them out of the conference.

The Network Executive
(November 2016, New England)

Once again, sitting at his desk, the Network Executive was happy. The Vodka was gone months ago. He poured himself a glass of Scotch. The second toast and drink was sweeter than the first. The beanstalk was cut, and the giant had fallen to his death. There would be no return for the Coach. The State University team had just beaten the Baptist University two years in a row. This second time was at home in Capitol City. They won by shutting down the Baptist University's high powered offense. On three different occasions, Baptist University was in the red zone and they came up empty every time – no touchdowns. He imagined the Booster doing cartwheels at the fifty yard line.

Once again, he pulled up a picture of the Coach on his laptop. He glared and said aloud,

"A man may kiss his wife, goodbye.

The rose may kiss a butterfly.

The beer may kiss the frosted glass.

And you, the coach, may kiss my ass."

He chuckled; he wished his wife would let him say this toast at the Thanksgiving dinner.

The Coach
(November 2016, Central Texas)

Watching events unfold and unable to do anything about them was like witnessing a train wreck in slow motion. The Coaching staff was clearly at war with the administration. Every member sent out the same tweet stating the truth of the sexual assault of the female athlete. The Coach understood why they did it. If he, the Coach, was not going to return, it was probable that none of the assistant coaches were going to return either. While he appreciated their support, it broke his general rule that the team came first. No individual- coach or player- should be greater than the team. He was disappointed in his former assistants.

When the coaching staff started fighting the administration, his players were hung out to dry. They did not receive proper direction or motivation. It showed during practices. It showed during the games. The football team lost five consecutive games they should have won. The play calling wasn't very good and the players lacked the fight they had had in the first six games when things mattered and there was still hope. Losing so many recruits played on their emotions and when every commitment from the 2017 recruiting class except one walked away, there was little hope for future success.

The Scapegoat

The Coach felt badly for the players. The coaching staff had messed up. Maybe at a time in the future, these coaches would apologize to the boys. Right now, however, they were all trying to figure out where they would work next year and how they were going to provide for their families.

For one game every season, the team had a "blackout" game. The uniforms were black: helmets, jerseys and pants. All the fans wore black. The Coach was given credit for such an innovative idea but he could not remember who came up with it originally. He read on the internet that fans had created a blackout T-shirt in honor of him. He was filled with emotion. He had 45,000 fans who loved him, but he still felt alone.

As he sat on a rocking chair on his deck, he reflected on the time he had spent in Central Texas. It was an honor to serve Baptist Nation. It was overwhelming to feel so adored. He was shaken. After all, like in so many institutions, it wasn't the innumerable fans who had sealed his fate. Rather, it had been a very small number of people with an immense amount of power, having private conversations about their hidden agendas behind closed doors.

The Advocate
(November 2016, Pacific Northwest)

The Advocate must have been outraged. It came with the responsibility of being the voice for the cause. She had power. Whatever she claimed became headlines. Whatever she wrote online was retweeted, reposted, or forwarded. When the Network needed her commentary, she was always available. She was now both a celebrity and a sexual assault expert.

She twisted the blackout tradition at the Baptist University and spun her own reasons behind it. When she found out that fans were buying and wearing black T-shirts with the Coach's initials, she called for the University to cancel the rest of its season. The media loved her rage.

She said the blackout game was re-victimizing the survivors. She called out and belittled the Coach by saying that he used his coaching staff to shield himself from being the last to know in off-field problems. The tradition of the blackout was cruelty. She even used the Commissioner's words of "institutional control." The ultimate slap in the face was her expression of gratitude that the Baptist University football team had taken a beating. No one, especially the university, was going to challenge her comments or reactions.

Her speaking engagements were on the uptick. Schools were lining up to sign her. They were willing to pay a lot of money to tell her story. Hypocrisy is an interesting creature. While the Advocate gladly accepted institutional money, she never bothered to read the annual security report from the schools where she spoke. If she would have read the reported crimes section, she would have discovered that there were more sexual assaults at those universities than there were at the Baptist University. The money, fame and power were so intoxicating, that she could not be troubled with the facts and the truth; people spewing their subjective opinions rarely are.

The Reporter
(November 2016, New England)

Sitting in her office, she glanced down at a desk calendar. She moved her favorite snow globe out of the way. Time had passed so quickly. The Reporter had been covering the story for over a year. She had the self-satisfaction of knowing she was instrumental in bringing to light a serious issue involving athletes and sexual assaults. She had successfully accomplished the storyline she set out to present: <u>The Baptist University purposely did not prevent sexual assaults for the sake of winning football games and the football coach created a culture that the "off the field" rules did not apply to his players.</u> The school and the Coach had been exposed. It would end with each pointing the finger at the other. And, she knew what finger they'd be pointing.

Now it was certain the Coach was never coming back to the Baptist University. The Reporter wanted to be prepared if the storyline changed. The lawsuit against the Coach and University was ongoing so she knew the story was far from over.

The Reporter had the Advocate in a strategic place. The Reporter felt a tiny bit of remorse for using her to assist the storyline, but the Network was giving her a lot of free publicity and her fees and speaking engagements were escalating. At the end of the day, they both benefited. It was an even trade. In addition to the Advocate, the Reporter also had the network beat writer down in Texas. This meant that any new surprise development that may occur would be covered promptly and consistent with the storyline. It was still her story. The beat writer was instructed to call her first with any news. The Reporter could easily draft an article for the Network if needed.

As she flipped thru the desk calendar, she started thinking about her goals for next year. There certainly was enough material to write a book. She had been contemplating the idea. No one had written an entire book on the scandal. The Writer's book only had a chapter highlighting the two trials of the football players. She had walked a tightrope by holding the Coach responsible, but not degrading him. If the Reporter was to write a book, she needed to make sure she did not disparage the Coach in case he coached elsewhere. If he landed a coaching job that was at one of the Network's favorite schools, it could present a problem.

She would focus on her book. If there were any new developments in the story, she could pick up right where she left off. The Writer in Capitol City had written her own book, so the Reporter would now write her own. She had been encouraged by the Network Executive after running the idea by him.

Besides writing her book, she wanted to find the next big story. The media attention was starting to decline on the Baptist University. The Reporter went back to focusing her crusade against the Catholic University. She had learned so much going through the trial transcripts from the Baptist University football player cases that she was confident she could apply what she had learned to future stories at different universities. She was preparing for her own lawsuit against the Catholic University. The case had been appealed to the state supreme court. She marked the important dates on a desk calendar. She was cautious not to count chickens. She was ready to start a sexual assault storyline for the Catholic University.

Grabbing the snow globe, she shook it and watched as the tiny white flakes went to the bottom. She thought about how ridiculous some of the Baptist University fans truly were. Many thought the University was targeted because they were Christians. What fools! They were targeted because there were two convictions. There was an empty Title IX office. Working with the FOIA requests was easy in Texas. The power of a grand jury facilitated the trial process. And, the University officials were unwilling to stand together. All the white flakes had settled to the bottom of the snow globe. A building with a golden dome was revealed. She still would rather have had the Catholic University be the central subject of her investigations. Her coverage of the Baptist University had nothing to do with belief systems. But it had much to do with perceived hypocrisy.

Tapping the top of the snow globe with her index finger, she was becoming more comfortable challenging God. She scribbled down. "Round 1 - God. Round 2- Me, Round 3 -TBD —-I have the edge".

The Coach
(December 2016, Central Texas)

The Coach was sitting on his deck rocker. The weather was colder than he had anticipated so he went inside to put on his barn coat. He returned to the deck again, but then decided to make coffee. Finally he sat back down on the rocker sipping his hot black coffee. He made the "are you kidding me" face when he noticed that he had poured the coffee into his Baptist University mug. He was antsy. He stood up, threw out the coffee and put the mug on the floor beside him. He needed to take a drive.

Ever since the Regents had released the articles to the newspapers at the end of October claiming the Coach was aware of certain sexual assaults by his players, the Coach wanted to know the source of the their information. It wasn't true-someone had lied. Back in May, before both parties signed the buyout settlement agreement, he requested the evidence the University upon which the University had relied. No information was ever given to him.

The newspaper articles contained new information, but it had never been presented to the Coach. He was at a loss as to what he should do. The language in the settlement agreement prevented him from making any disparaging remarks about the University. So he contacted his former employer and asked them to provide the information again. If they could not provide the documents, then he requested that they retract the articles. The university did neither and never responded.

The Coach was taping his fingers against the dashboard deep in thought. He felt like he was in a rut. He needed a game plan. Everybody knows somebody who knows somebody. He was starting to get some phone calls about the possibilities of coaching again. The initial calls were being placed by boosters from other Power 5 conference schools. All the calls were considered "unofficial," but the boosters wanted to gauge the coach's level of interest in coaching at each of their schools. Yes, the Coach was very interested.

Three problems immediately arose when the conversations started to proceed to the "next step" of the hiring process. The first problem was the hiring schools wanted the Coach's response in regards to the Baptist University administration reporting that they had found nineteen football players involved in seventeen sexual assaults. The second problem was that the hiring schools wanted to know the status and sometimes details of the lawsuit in which the Coach was named. The third problem was the media attention. As soon as it was mentioned publicly that a university was considering interviewing the Coach, the media pounced and lambasted the Coach and that university for considering him as coach. In every case, the hiring school would respond that they were not considering the Coach at this time.

The Coach was unable to respond, legally and contractually, to any of the questions. He pulled his truck over on the side of the road. He called his friend and personal attorney. The two men decided his only option was to file a lawsuit against the three Regents who provided interviews and information to the media. He wanted the source of the information that was the basis of the released articles. This source of information was preventing him from finding new employment.

The puritan woman caught in an adulterous relationship was forced to wear a Scarlet A in Nathaniel Hawthorne's legendary book. The Coach felt he had such an emblem (SA just for Sexual Assault) branded on him. Nobody was willing to hire him. Nobody was willing to research the facts. Nobody was willing to speak for him. He had done nothing wrong and nobody cared.

The FCS AD

(December 2016, Two states away from Texas)

The AD was looking over the statistics of his football program in his small corner office of the athletic building. Over the last ten years they only had had two winning seasons. Neither of those had double digit wins. Both bowl appearances ended up in losses. The stadium was half empty. At every home game, they had to give away half the tickets just to make the stadium look somewhat full. There was no network contract. On a rare occasion, they would they have a game televised only if they agreed to be a "blood donor" for the perennial powerhouse opponent. "We suck," he said loudly to himself and his door was open so others down the hall heard him.

The AD did not have a temper but he was bold and rarely employed a "filter" to express his point of view. He was a bottom-line guy and even though he liked details, he did not want to spend any time in flowery talk or surface conversations. He valued hard work and honesty. He liked to have fun, but his motto was "work hard-play hard," and in that order. He was a former college player and had been a defensive strong safety who loved to knock the crap out anybody wearing an opposing jersey. He "walked on" his first year. He only played special teams his second year. He finally earned a scholarship only to retire a season later after two knee surgeries on the same knee. He would tell people that he could sense when the weather was about to change, with his bum knee.

Unlike FBS schools where football generated enough revenue to pay the bills for all the sports and the athletic department, at his school, football barely broke even. In college football it is the story of the haves and the have-nots. The haves made a lot of money. The have-nots barely cut it. It angered the AD that the Network decided who would in which camp. The AD hated the Network. Life was not fair, he knew that fact but he could not stand when life privileged others.

The AD had been following the story of the Coach since the lawsuit was filed in March 2016. The story intrigued him, but something about all of it seemed incredibly wrong and unjust. He could not put his finger on it; kind of like having a dead mouse in the kitchen that you can smell but not see. He liked the coach. The Coach-a cross between Robert Duvall and John Wayne; was confident but humble. The AD loved the Coach's mission focus too.

The AD knew the Coach could help his FCS program and school tremendously. A spread offense could put fifty points on the scoreboard on a Saturday afternoon and would give the program the boost it needed. He wanted to hire the Coach. The AD was a contrarian and bought when others were selling. And now was the time "to buy" and hire the Coach. The AD knew that even though the President of FCS University was from Texas and loved football, it would be an uphill battle.

The AD called the FCS President and started the conversation by saying, "I've got a solution for our football program." The AD was leaning back in his office chair with both feet on the desk

The President responded, '"Well, if you know how we are going to get three more wins with only one more game to play, I'm all ears."

It was a good to hear the President be in a joking mood. "Maybe next year, we'll do even better," the AD said. He paused briefly doubting in his mind what he'd just said, "I know how we are going to get better in the future. I want to hire the coach from the Baptist University."

"That's a good one," the President snorted. "Should we go ahead and lower our ACT composite score to 7 while we're at it?" He had a tendency to laugh at his own jokes.

"Fantastic. I'm going to call him tomorrow," the AD quickly added. He was hoping to catch the President off guard.

There was a longer pause before the President said, "You're seriously considering this hire?"

"Damn right," said the AD. "I doubt we can get him. I would be a fool not to try to get one of the greatest offensive minds and successful coaches in college football. Right now, it's a soft market and I want to act today."

"Why would I want to bring the media circus to my campus?" the President asked.

"Because he knows how to win football games," replied the AD.

"Well, according to the papers he knows more than just football," the President added.

"Just hear me out," the AD said. The AD knew he had to build a case.

"Do you have a list of candidates?," asked the President.

"Yes," the AD replied.

The President continued, "Then go to the next one on the list."

AD responded, "Mr. President…."

The President interrupted, "Next!" His sense of humor had evaporated.

"What if I can show you that he did nothing wrong?" hurried the AD.

"Is he still being sued?" the President asked. He ignored the AD's request.

"Yes," said the AD

"Don't mention it to me again until the suit is settled. I'll give you *your* day in court only because I'm curious. FYI – you have about a five percent chance of getting my approval. You are only getting the five percent for the curiosity factor."

"Works for me," said the AD. In his mind he was thinking "Damn".

Five percent was better than none, but the AD knew he had better continue his due diligence.

The Coach
(Late January, 2017, Central Texas)

The only correspondence the Coach had with the Regents was through his attorney. But the Coach still wanted to see the documents that the University had used to draft the separation and settlement agreement. He continued to have a dialogue with a couple of the donors, both of whom had relationships with some of Regents. These donors were capable of getting some information – albeit, vague.

On a trip to Big D, he met one of the donors at a downtown bar-b-que restaurant. During their lunch of beef ribs, the donor told the Coach that he had heard that some of the information the Regents had discovered was damaging. The donor did not have any details, but he told the Coach to proceed with caution. How the information was presented, along with the content, could seriously harm the Coach.

On the drive back to Central Texas, the Coach thought that if there was damaging information, why did the Regents not release or provide it to him when he had asked back in May 2016? Why would they agree to settle with him if they had details that would give them just cause? Nothing made sense. It weighed heavy on him, but was about to get heavier.

The Coach got a phone call from his longtime friend and Assistant Coach who informed him that he was going to file a defamation suit against Baptist University. Because of their friendship, both men had decided not to talk to each other during the Coach's lawsuit. If depositions were served, they wanted to be able to say that they had not talked about the case. The Assistant Coach just broke that silence.

"I wanted to let you know I was filing my own lawsuit against the University," the Assistant Coach said. "There was never a single complaint about how I did my job. Now nobody is willing to hire me because of the termination."

The Coach told his friend, "Do what you need to do. You have to be able to provide and take care of your family." The Coach knew his friend needed support, and could tell the Assistant Coach was getting anxious about his future.

The Assistant Coach said, "I have asked why I was fired. The Regents were told by the law firm that I was uncooperative and not helpful during their investigation, so I'm naming them in the suit as well. The football operations duties were hard enough, let alone trying to babysit a hundred-something players. It is not right." His termination from Baptist University made him "untouchable" to all other schools. The Coach had never heard his friend complain. And even though he didn't admire complaints, he let it go because he knew what the pressure felt like.

"I am sorry," said the Coach. "I'll write a recommendation for you, but you know I'm not the most popular guy in the world right now. Being thrown under the bus, and then having it back up on you is a tough place to be," replied the Coach. He was trying to offer encouragement.

The Assistant Coach said, "I know," and then he paused.

The Coach added, "Look there is no one else in the world I trust more than you. You went beyond the call of duty as a friend for over twenty years. I know you protected me even when I did not know I was being protected. I am forever grateful. I know you would take a bullet for me if needed. You were the very best."

"Thanks Coach," said the Assistant. "What do you think of my suit?"

The Coach said, "Be careful. The Regents have gone to great lengths to separate themselves from the football program. There is a reason we were never shown the detailed information behind the printed Findings of Facts. You should know that I'm going to dismiss my lawsuit. The 'unknown' is a heavy burden on me; I'm not sleeping much these days. Right now I need more peace in my life."

"Hmmmm," sounded the Assistant Coach. "I'm going to proceed, I'm living off savings now, and I need to start getting a paycheck. I'm un-hirable. Football operations are all I know, and I'm good at it. I'll keep you posted if any new information comes up during the discovery phase of the suit."

"I appreciate it, you are a good friend. Good luck," said the Coach.

"Is there any way my filing could hurt, you Coach?" asked the Assistant.

"No, I am good. I'll be fine. Go give a whooping," encouraged the Coach. It had been a long time since the Coach had been able to open his own can of whoop ass.

These were famous last fighting words, as the worst was yet to come.

The Regents
(Late January 2017, Central Texas)

The Regents were slowly making their way through the pile of lawsuits and accusations. The Assistant Coach's suit alleging defamation by the Regents caught them off guard. The timing was oddly coincidental with another lawsuit filed by a familiar attorney.

 In some incidences, the school settled with some victims before suits were even filed. Other suits were settled soon after filing. The Regents truly thought the worst was behind them until the renowned Title IX attorney, who represented the victim from the Transfer Player's sexual assault, had filed another new lawsuit. This new action was so full of allegations, that it shocked the Regents, and the media had a hay day with it.

The filing was based on a sexual assault that had already been investigated by the university. The players were deemed guilty by the school and expelled. Recently, a Grand Jury indicted the players with criminal convictions. But this new suit was a money grab by the same victim who told the police that no sexual assault had occurred.

When a suit claims that fifty-two sexual assaults were done by thirty plus football players, the allegations make every media publication's headline. The suit claimed the football team had a hostess program where in the girls were encouraged to show players a "good time." It claimed that coaches made sexual and racial innuendoes about white girls liking black players. Ironically, the Coach was not listed in this as a defendant on the suit, the victim's attorney generally named coaches personally in his cases.

Upstairs in the boardroom of the administration building at the Baptist University, thirty plus Regents gathered. No one said a word. A powerful group of successful businessmen, attorneys and pastors, none of whom ever felt more defeated. They had spent the last six months uncovering nineteen sexual assaults and now the world was going to hear about allegations of fifty-two. It gave the appearance that they were either trying to hide the number of suits or that they were incapable of discovering all the sexual assault incidents that had taken place on their watches, at their school.

One of the pastors stood up. "Fellas, let's get to work. Nothing is going to happen if we sit here feeling sorry for ourselves." It was difficult to be positive. There were entirely too many clouds and not a stitch of silver.

One of the Regents who had been sued personally by the Assistant Coach, said "First order of business is to kick the teeth out of the damn Assistant Coach. Get me a response." He was pissed and ready for a fight; then someone handed him a stack of stapled documents

The Regents had been preparing a response to the Coach's defamation lawsuit, but he had dropped. The Regents simply changed that response to address the claim from the Assistant Coach, which included texts exchanged between the Coach and the Assistant Coach. There were exchanges that involved players involved and drugs, brandishing guns, and exposing themselves publically. No sexual assaults were mentioned. Anyone reading the response would wonder whether the Regents other information on the Coach?

This response would show the Commissioner that the Regents knew how to implement institutional control.

(Note: Generally speaking, lawyers don't sue people; people sue people. And a lawsuit begins with filing a petition, which is a collection of allegations. Each allegation in a petition is just that – an allegation. The allegations ought to be provable and true, but often aren't. But they make good theatre because they are public documents and are often wildly untrue, and only one side of the story. Trials are supposed to get to the truth, but even the rules of evidence often prevent the truth from being known.)

The Commissioner
(February 2017, Big D, Texas)

The Conference Executive Committee had an emergency meeting to discuss the Baptist University situation. The three members all flew into Big D. In a meeting room at the conference headquarters, they were in agreement about their recommendation to the rest of the conference presidents.

The Commissioner did not even bother to call the Regent this time. It would only upset him further. The conference voted. There was a motion to remove the Baptist University from the conference. Since they had just voted not to add two new teams, primarily due to the Network's strong objection, finding a team, at this point, to replace the Baptist University would be problematic. Plus, the Baptist University was not going to just write a check for forty-six million dollars. If pushed out, the conference would be tied up in courts for years and scheduling would be a mess. Further, the other teams in the conference did not want to be subjected to investigations, in the event the Baptist University tried to prove that it was no different than the other schools, when it came to the epidemic of campus sexual assaults.

The vote was unanimous. The conference voted to withhold six million dollars in broadcasting revenue from the Baptist school until it could get institutional control. The amount was equal to the first broadcasting revenue payment that the conference schools received annually from the Network. Every conference member was texting its athletic department to schedule the Baptist University for each of their homecoming weekends.

The Commissioner had never seen the two state school presidents smile as wide as they were smiling now. It almost seemed that they delighted in this punishment of their conference opponent down Baptist way. Goal #2? Once again was accomplished.

The Network Executive
(February 2017, New England)

The Network Executive was sitting in his home office. He looked at the events over the past year. Things could not have gone better. Actually, they'd gone better than he originally thought. He loved the idea that six million dollars of revenue was being held in escrow until the Baptist University could demonstrate institutional control. That the Baptist University could not immediately get its distribution was like a final kick in the midsection. The Network Executive did not want them to be kicked out of the conference, but they needed to be returned to irrelevancy, like so many years in the past. They needed to go back and be the doormat. They would be the football doormat of the conference once again. He did not care if they did well in track, women's basketball, or tennis. Who cares about those sports? He laughed at the thought of paying to broadcast equestrian contests.

The Network Executive thought the State University's choice for its new head coach was outstanding. He had a winning tradition, fight and he could recruit. The choice should impact positively the investment in the exclusive State University Network.

The media was a powerful force, and he controlled it. He grabbed the ruler inside the middle desk drawer and held it out in front of him. He remembered the line from a Mel Brooks movie: "It's great to be the king." He was the king. Looking at the ruler was metaphorically humorous to him.

The FCS AD

(February 2017, Two states away from Texas)

He was walking across campus when his phone signaled that he had received an email. The email was from the President and the subject line read, "52 cases of rape by 31 players." The AD was hurrying to climb the steps up to his office to get online. On every other step, he let a different expletive fly.

After swallowing three or four ibuprofen for his bad knee, the AD responded to his President. The AD had already started his homework and was making phone calls; he had checked LinkedIn and discovered that one of his friend's daughters was part of the hostess program at the Baptist University, so he called his friend to get the scoop on her experience.

The AD responded with an email. "Total BS. I know somebody with a daughter in the program. They were explicitly told not to have any kind of sexual contact with players but she did say that some of her friends hung out with the players after they enrolled as college students. Most of the time, they stayed with the high school recruiting candidates on the sideline." If they were "having a good time" he was pretty sure 45,000 people there in the stadium would have noticed. The only culture that Coach produced was a winning culture.

The President replied. "I am troubled by the text exchanges. I still say move on to the next candidate."

The AD wrote back, "Give it more time." His gut and his instincts told him that the Coach was the right guy to hire. The AD just needed more information to strengthen his argument.

The Advocate
(Late February 2017, Pacific Northwest)

She had gotten used to being "online" all day, every day. The Advocate was getting flooded with attacks and rebuttals from the Baptist University fans and alums. She referred to them as trolls. If they thought she was going to move her spotlight to another university, the "trolls" were in for a major disappointment. It was no longer about seeing the Coach exiled; he was gone. She would now expose the culture. The Coach was gone, the president was gone, the coaching staff was gone, and the troublesome players were gone. So now it was the culture she needed to attack.

When the Baptist University women's basketball coach stood up for the university during a press conference, the Advocate decided to challenge her. It was time for a fight. The basketball coach was so worn out by all the media attention that had been put on the school, she voiced her opinion that it was time for the media to move on to another story.

The Advocate had learned the meaning and the power behind the word "alleged." She reminded the public through her blogs and tweets that there were "52 alleged rapes" that had happened while the Coach was there. How dare the basketball women's coach defend the university? The Advocate would decide when it was time to move on, not the coach. *She* was the voice. After all, the NCAA was considering appointing her to its Sexual Assault Committee.   As her voice became stronger, her influential power grew as well.

The Coach

(March 2017, Central Texas)

It was simple. It was sincere. His mama's words, "Do the right thing" came to mind. But when you are alone in the wilderness, no one can hear you. The Coach was prevented from speaking, so no one could listen. In order to be heard, his words had to be read. The Coach wrote a letter. In his letter he testified:

- I never covered up any sexual violence
- I never had any contact with anyone that claimed to be a victim
- I promoted excellence but never at the sacrifice of safety
- I never obstructed justice
- When I was alerted about any sexual assault incident, I always said to report it and the attacker should be punished.

It was so simple. He just wanted to clear his name and be able to coach again.

The FCS AD

(March 2017, Two states away from Texas)

The AD forwarded the letter the Coach had written to the President and followed up with a phone call to his office.

"What do you think of the letter?," asked the AD.

There was a long pause on the other end of the line. The President said, "I believe him."

The AD silently fist pumped the air, and said, "And...?"

The President responded, "The texts still trouble me. Guns, drugs, exposing... ."

The AD said, "Mr. President, I don't need to tell you the background of a lot of these players. Several come from single parent homes and are poor. Many are exposed to drugs, guns and promiscuity. Now, you are going to take them out of *that* environment and expect them to change overnight just because they suddenly find themselves at higher education institutions with predominantly white middle class students? Every psychologist will tell you behavior is nurture versus nature: genetics and how kids are raised!" He spoke with authority but he kept a "matter of fact" tone.

The President, choosing his words carefully, asked "Hypothetically, is this going on at every school across the country?"

The AD said, "It is. The NCAA is never going to take a stand against it because given the kids we're talking about; it will come across as racism. The truth is, if college football-or sports, period- gives these guys a chance to better their lives and improve their communities? I am in favor of recruiting guys who have grown up in that environment." He silently hoped the President wouldn't ask any questions regarding some of their own players' backgrounds. It was true. The AD was a firm believer in athletic scholarships; his regret was that there weren't more scholarships to hand out.

The President said, "I still have no interest in this guy until the lawsuit is settled. If we find out the victim has *actual* evidence, then I'm not interested. We do not want to open the door to this only to find out there is another suit and then having to pay a contract severance. I'll say this...you are up to twenty percent -. I'm past the curiosity stage".

The AD did not believe in luck. He would have to study all the angles involved in this hiring. He would have to find out exactly what happened to the Coach at Baptist University. He was determined. Things would have to fall into place. He grabbed the football shaped stressed ball off his desk and squeezed it as hard as could. Pretending the stress ball was a set of dice, he rolled it

on his desk as the thought raced through his mind:
"Winner winner, chicken dinner."

The Network Executive
(March 2017, New England)

He thought his rule about drinking only before 5:00 PM for celebratory reasons was a stupid one. The Network Executive was about to break it again. He poured himself a double of whiskey. The executive memo he had just read made him ill.

The Network was still making money. He liked thinking they were a cash cow for the parent corporation. But the loss of ten million subscribers in four years, and a couple hundred thousand each new month, was staggering. Could those numbers be right? College football was still the most popular ticket. Did people really care if the parent company was making shifts to the political left? It was still football, damn it. He needed to see the market financials from the state of Texas. He needed to know if that market was experiencing the same trends as the rest of the country. What was happening down there?

He took another sip of whiskey. It left him dissatisfied-this was no thing to celebrate.

Lane Alpert

The Coach
(Early April – Central Texas)

The Coach walked outside when he heard a car pull up in his driveway. He offered his former assistant a glass of lemonade, but he refused. This was just a short personal visit from his friend. The Assistant Coach had stopped by to let the Coach know that he had lost the suit against the Regents. The worst part of it was that he had to pay court costs and attorney fees. His house was up for sale. He apologized that his suit brought the texts into the public arena. If he ever did get a job again, he was never going to use a university issued phone. He apologized once more and then as he prepared to leave, the Coach gave him a hug for encouragement and patted him on the back.

But before he left, he gave the Coach a crinkled 9x12 Brown Kraft envelope. The Assistant Coach had some information he wanted the Coach to have. He had made notes some three months prior after his dinner with the Staff Writer. He had researched and gathered some additional information too. He had made a handful of copies. He thought it might be helpful in the Coach's lawsuit. Then, he thanked the Coach; someone had paid his mortgage for the last six months. Deep down, the Assistant Coach knew it was Coach but he did not ask and the Coach did not say. Besides, the Coach was the kind of guy who would deny it anyway.

As the Assistant coach backed out of the driveway, he waved. The Coach just gave him thumbs up as he bit the inside of his mouth on purpose. He fought back the tears. So many people had been hurt as a result of this entire ordeal.

The Network Executive
(Late April 2017, New England)

The halls of the entire building were solemn. There was a silent awkwardness as people milled about, unsure what they could say to their former associates and employees. The Network's commitment to professional football and basketball along with college football had resulted in skyrocketing broadcasting costs. The parent company had seen enormous decline from the previous year's numbers in all respects. A memo went out: deep staff cuts were imminent across the organization. But the investigative unit only had one layoff. The Network Executive was also sorry to release the beat writer in Capitol City, Texas. Cable was losing the battle to live streaming. The Network would adjust, and rebound like it always had. But seeing so many longtime employees and friends leave never got easier. But hey – this was business.

He needed several drinks just to face people. But he would delay heading home to avoid as many as possible. The pit in his stomach over the terminations would remain – no doubt about it: this had been an awful day.

The FCS AD

(April 2017, Two states away from Texas)

The Coach's trial was not over, but the AD wanted to run some things by the President over the phone.

The President looked at the caller ID and saw that it was the AD. The first words out of his mouth were, "The trial is not over." The AD was so committed to this, but the President couldn't waiver.

"I know," answered the AD," but I want to run things past you to make sure my logic makes sense."

"OK," said the President. He was a good listener.

The AD started, "Point One: The scandal at the Baptist University is all about sexual assault, correct?"

"Correct," said the President, unsure where the conversation was heading.

The AD continued. "So, if the University had solid evidence on the Coach, it would have just enacted a cause to terminate, right?"

The President agreed.

"But they did not terminate; instead they executed a buyout agreement with a gag order to prevent disparaging remarks, and the truth from coming out, correct?"

"Yes." The President was impressed with the AD's fortitude to keep pursuing the possible hire.

The AD continued, "The number one investigative reporter from the Network, who worked on this story for a year and half and who had all of the FOIA information including police reports, trial transcripts and evidentiary documents could not find the Coach's behavior or his actions contrary to any of the points the Coach made in his letter."

That was compelling to the President. "Go on... ."

The AD stated, "The first lawsuit was the only one in which the Coach was named personally, but on a negligence charge. We both know why he can't be sued under Title IX. The other suits did not name him. Why was that? Because there was no concrete evidence, all the information was hearsay, opinion and conjecture."

"Anything else?" the President asked.

"Every derogatory headline about the Coach came from lawsuit allegations or the Advocate's quotes.. Headlines sell papers. Headlines spin stories. So if the headlines are from allegations in the lawsuits, there is no slander. There is no libel. There is no recourse. What jerk is willing to challenge the words of alleged rape victims, much less, actual ones?"

"No one;" the President said stoically.

"So if someone is unable to speak for him or herself and the media is unwilling to present all sides, and the University never comments, then only one side of the story gets told," the AD concluded.

"Welcome to journalism," the President uttered. But the AD's point wasn't lost on him.

The AD continued, "So here are my points:

1. The Reporter got all of the police reports.

2. She had complete rosters because, that's what she used to make her FOIA requests.

3. All the players are on social media – Facebook, Instagram, Snapchat.

4. All the players are no longer students at Baptist University.

Why aren't there any interviews with teammates of the guys convicted or listed in the police reports? Only a handful of players are in the NFL now, so it can't be reputational risk at stake or fear of damaging their broadcast brand. Why not go after the folks who created the culture? At the end of the day, how can anyone be responsible for another person's actions? The Coach cannot control every player's "off the field" actions, just like you cannot possibly control mine, even though I report to you."

The President was mentally searching for holes in the AD's argument. There had to be something missing. If both he and the AD could arrive at this conclusion, then why couldn't others? Unless, of course, the conclusion was formed prior to the investigation– prior to looking at the evidence – the conclusion they did not want reach? Quietly he replied "AD, you are right." Then a little bit louder – "You are right. Damn you. You are right." The President had one more question. "Why not bring him back in a year; why hire a new coach?"

"My thoughts exactly! I need more time to figure that one out," replied the AD.

The President said, "It's still a no-go for me while he's in the lawsuit. The risk is just too great."

"Yes, Sir," the AD answered.

"You're at fifty percent. Good work." The President hung up thinking to himself, "Just maybe… ."

The AD felt a strange movement in his bum knee. Could his knee be signaling another sign of change? Nah, There was probably just a rain storm on the way.

The Writer

(Early May 2017, Capitol City Texas)

The Writer had just finished her speech at the Women's Sports Media group. She was thankful the venue was held in a hotel in Capitol City, Texas this year. The panel for the meeting included The Reporter and the Advocate. She had a lot of respect for both of them. They were instrumental in the development and continuation of the Baptist University "scandal." All the presentations and the follow up questions featured their involvement in exposing Baptist University. In some ways, it felt like the chapter was over. She was going to miss it terribly

The Writer was surprised to see the Software Developer waiting for her in the back of the room. Since it was a women's association, any male instantly stood out. Knowing his sexual preference, she jokingly said, "If you're looking for a date, boy did you come to the wrong place."

"Ha Ha," he said factiously, though with seriousness. "We need to talk." He led her behind a column so they could talk in private. "I have something that is going make your day, maybe even your year. Get ready for round two."

The Software Developer was talking so fast that the Writer was having trouble keeping up. She jumped to a conclusion, and asked, "The trial of the Tall Defensive Player from the Baptist University has begun?" She thought a new trial involving another football player was underway.

"No," he said. "I have another story. It involves another school." His voice volume was above a whisper.

The Writer had set an alert in her internet web browser to receive a notification every time a college sexual assault news article hit the internet. The Writer was perplexed. "I haven't seen any new trials or convictions hit my radar screen. What have you got?"

"At first I was scared. One of our boosters contacted me and said he had a job for me. I thought it was a programming project. He gave me a list of players at another school in our conference and asked if I would put together a 'questionable character' list for that school, like the one I did about the Coach of the Baptist University. He is going to pay me for it and he gave some other instructions as well, but he would like *you* to break the story when it happens."

"How did he get my name?" the Writer asked. She wondered why he hadn't contacted her directly.

"He was familiar with your article in 2015 and the book you wrote. He wants you to handle this project too.

The Writer asked, "Is it another school in Texas?" She was already thinking about which magazine would work best. Her interest was certainly piqued. And this "send a messenger" way of contacting her made it seem like a big deal.

"No, it's the Other State University in our conference," the Software Developer answered.

"No way?! Count me in!'" said the Writer. If this was true, and the story featured the Other State University, this could be award-winning. On her way home she stopped at the local convenience store and bought a couple of pre-paid cell phones, just in case. The thought of needing to be anonymous was thrilling to her.

The Regents

(Mid-May 2017, Central Texas)

There was a time for cooler heads to prevail, but the Regents were well beyond that point. They had run out of others to blame, so they started pointing fingers at each other. Not all of them were displaying the same finger.

Another new lawsuit had been filed but the incident was familiar – the events that lead the coaching staff to cross the administration. This one involved a female athlete who was purportedly "gang raped" by some of the football players. It was the incident where the Coach had first been made aware by the women's volleyball coach. Once again, the victim had not wanted to press charges, even though the head coach advised that it would be the best course of action. It was the incident that the three Regents had released to the press the previous October, the same one in which they alluded that the Coach knew about a sexual assault but had failed to notify Judicial Affairs.

Some of the Regents had expected this suit to come to fruition. It was one of the seventeen cases they already knew about. But other Regents blamed the three, who had spoken to the media prematurely. They felt that had they not done interviews and brought it to the press, the suit would never have happened. Once again, the facts showed that the Coach had urged the victims to press charges because there was no Title IX process in place at that time.

And, once again, The Coach was not named in the suit. Allegations still swirled that it was the Coach's culture that was the root of the problem. The female athlete's coach, whom the student first told about the assault, was also not named in the suit. It was more than irony that the only suit, which named the Coach was the first lawsuit filed. Over a year had passed since that first suit; more information had been released and reported since that time. Yet the Coach was never named in any of the other lawsuits filed against the University.

The Regents closed their meeting in prayer. Many of them prayed silently that the Commissioner would not hold back another six million dollars of the broadcast money.

The Reporter
(May 2017, New England)

Her voicemail at her desk was full. The speaking engagement requests seemed to be endless. The Reporter was the keynote speaker at many associations and conventions. She knew she was giving away a lot of her trade secrets for uncovering stories every time she spoke. She was okay with sharing the tips because she still knew how to find the *big* story and how to catch the big fish.

She was in the middle of writing her book which she found exhilarating. It was a welcome change from the articles she wrote for the investigative unit. She had a mountain of information and so the writing went quickly. Chapters were being completed daily it seemed. The only major disappoint was that none of the lawsuits revealed any concrete information that the Coach had done anything wrong involving any of his players' alleged sexual assaults. She wondered why the Network Executive was so focused on wanting to make a connection. The best they were able to do was to infer that the Coach had promoted a culture of unaccountability among his football players. The story was that the *school* had let the victims down. To the Reporter, it really did not matter. A published book was a nice reward. Watching the Baptist University fall from greatness, at least primarily because of her efforts, was just a bonus.

She was being challenged to find the "next Baptist University." Her personal lawsuits against other universities were making it difficult to break the next story. In two different states, her cases against the universities and their police departments were making their way to the respective state Supreme Courts. She had won her cases in both of the lower courts in Michigan. And she even won a follow-up suit wherein the judge ruled that the school was required to pay her attorney's fees. The school had appealed to the highest state court. She was certain they would rule in favor of her as well. It would have been easier if they just gave her the requested information in the first place.

The Catholic University case was still heading to the Indiana Supreme Court. She tapped the top of the snow globe again. One of these days, she promised that she would go after them. She was patient. She had a lot to show for her effort and skill over this past year.

Since she was still keeping score, she tried to see if there was a connection between God and the school in Michigan. She was unable to find one. Maybe it was just neutral territory. No worries. She knew there would be other opportunities down the road to challenge Him. She was confident.

The Coach
(May 2017, Central Texas)

Apparently some of the information the Assistant Coach discovered was more than noteworthy. The Coach had given it to his own attorney. It was insightful and legally relevant. The lawsuit against the Coach was progressing. Both the plaintiff and the defendants were awaiting a judge's decision on a particular issue: whether the detailed information that law firm created in its Finding of Facts would be admissible in court. Had the defense lost its attorney-client privileges when it created the Finding of Facts? Had it lost the same privilege when it responded to the Assistant Coach's defamation lawsuit? His ruling could have a dramatic influence on all of the university's pending cases.

The Coach and the Regents decided to bury the hatchet with one another for a while. The Coach was fielding calls about open coaching positions. But he needed something to validate that he had done nothing wrong. No one in the public believed him. Not a single media outlet had tried to support him.

The Coach decided to share, with the University, the Assistant Coach's information. In exchange for sharing the information, the Baptist University's in-house counsel drafted and signed a letter stating that the

Coach had no knowledge about or direct contact with any sexual assault victims. It read as follows:

"Dear Coach:

We read with interest the letter you wrote to Baptist Nation back in March of this year. While certain information has been revealed in the context of pending litigation, your letter underscores the fact we have been unable to share all of the information developed during the law firm's investigation.

We appreciate the spirit and tone of your message to Baptist Nation in support of the University's efforts to address sexual violence and the ongoing healing process within our community. As the University continues to respond to various investigations and lawsuits, your continued cooperation in sharing honestly and completely the facts of which you are aware will be of great importance.

As you speak with others regarding these issues, you can be assured you make certain statements without fear of contradiction from Baptist University based on the information currently known to us. In particular, at this time we are unaware of any situation where you personally had contact with anyone who directly reported to you being the victim of sexual assault or that you directly discouraged the victim of an alleged sexual assault from reporting to law enforcement or the University's administration. Nor are we aware of any situation where you played a student athlete who had been found responsible for sexual assault.

We wish the best in your future endeavors.

Very truly yours,

Baptist University"

Finally he had a document to show potential employers that he had done nothing wrong. He read and re-read the letter to make sure it was real and accurate. He made a couple copies in case one was lost. And he sent one to his agent. It was the first bright moment he had experienced in well over a year.

The FCS AD

(May 2017, Two states away from Texas)

Each month that passed meant the Coach's lawsuit was either close to settling or going to trial. The main concern the FCS AD had was that if it went to trial, the judge could set a court date next year sometime, thereby delaying any contract he could offer the Coach.

He was tossing the stress football up in the air when he called the President to circle back and pick up the conversation where it had left off.

The President asked, "How is our project coming along?" He was fascinated with the discovery information the AD had provided so far.

The AD loved how he used the word "our." "*We* have hit an impasse," the AD said.

"Where?" asked the President, with noticeable concern.

"You asked the question last time, "Why did the Baptist University just not re-hire him in a year?" We agreed that it would have been a great strategic plan. I can only come up with three possible scenarios."

"Which are?" The President was curious.

"First, the Regents did not have any sexual assault information at first and they were waiting to see if any evidence would develop? Then, if evidence developed they could terminate the Coach with cause," stated the AD.

The President, playing devil's advocate said, "Then why settle with a gag order a month later with the 'intent to fire' announcement? Also, there had already been enough information to fire the two staffers back in May. They found seventeen cases involving nineteen players."

The AD added, "And the female athlete case, the latest lawsuit, was released at the end of October. We don't know when they discovered that information. But, that case still supports Coach's view that of no direct contact coupled with the encouragement for victims to press charges.

The second scenario for not re-hiring is if a small faction or the Board wanted the Coach gone permanently. What if a couple Regents went 'off the reservation" and acted on their own. The ones that were interviewed were the same point people for the law firm investigation."

The President was that thinking long and hard. "Let's come back to that possibility. What else?"

"The third scenario was something happened to cause the Regents to purposely change their strategy of a one year suspension," he continued to toss his football in the air.

The President said, "Do you have a hypothesis why they changed their strategy?"

"Yes, but it is not a why; it's a *who*. I have a couple suspects but give me more time." The AD snagged the stress ball out of mid toss.

Both men were like two little kids trying to solve a puzzle. They did not know whether all the pieces of the puzzle were in the box.

The Commissioner
(May 2017, Big D Texas)

As he was walked down the hall toward his office, the Commissioner wondered why his assistant wished him happy birthday. His birthday was four months ago. He was surprised when he opened his office door. On his desk was an overstuffed 10 x 13 brown Kraft envelope. It had a handwritten address and return address, and someone had used postage stamps in the upper right corner. It was addressed to him personally. The return address said "Ronald McDonald," which he thought was strange. He was cautious before opening the package. The Commissioner googled the address and it was actually the hamburger restaurant located in Capitol City, Texas. On the outside of the envelope, someone had written in black sharpie, "Happy Birthday."

When he opened the envelope, his stomach dropped, and for a split second he thought he was going to be sick. He could not believe what he was seeing. This could not be happening all over again? Could it? He thought he was being bribed, except that the letter read:

"Dear Commissioner:

The Scapegoat

This is not a bribe. Since you had so much fun handling the Baptist University scandal, I thought you would enjoy another. I just wanted you to know about it first so you will be better prepared this time. I have researched another school at this time. In a three year period the school reported over fifty sexual assaults. As you know, 1) this does not include any sexual assaults that would be considered 'off campus' and reported by the municipal police department. 2) Eighty percent of the time, sexual assaults go unreported.

"During this period of time this particular school had twenty-eight players leave the program. Twenty of the players transferred to other schools to continue their college football careers. And most of those transfers were to schools where they would not have to sit out a year. The other eight have not surfaced at other schools yet, so their whereabouts are currently unknown. I am not going to give them the benefit of doubt that they could not handle the high academic standards of the university, just look at all the other nitwits who have shown they could graduate there. Do you know if they are in jail?

"You and I are going to find out together how many of those twenty-eight players made up those fifty sexual assaults plus any new ones that will come out of the woodwork. Also, there were twenty-three players who were arrested in a five year period. We will see where those arrests lead us. I look forward to working with you. If we have fun on this project, we have eight more schools to work with as well. I have sped up the process so that it won't drag for over a year like the story of those irrelevant buffoons at Baptist University. Since my list is not exhaustive like the Network's Reporter, I have already done my fishing, and am hoping that the information requests will go more smoothly. So I have enclosed copies of the following:

1) The university's annual security report for three years
2) A List of the twenty-eight football players who have washed out of the program.
3) A Copy of the FOIA request to the municipal police department.
4) A Copy of the FOIA request to the campus police department.
5) A Copy of the FOIA request to the Director of Judicial Affairs.
6) A Copy of the FOIA request to school president.
7) A Copy of the FOIA request to the state's attorney general.
8) A Copy of the FOIA request for NCAA compliance transfer request for each of the players who transferred.
9) A Copy of the letter sent to the Writer, outlining the project.
10) A Copy of the letter sent to The Advocate, outlining the project.
11) A Copy of the letter sent to the famous Title IX attorney
12) A Copy of the purchase order for Facebook and LinkedIn advertisements.

Do we really want to stop campus sexual violence in the conference or is it more fun to just talk about it?

You decide.

Ronald McDonald"

"That's all."

The Commissioner just sat and stared. He was angry. It sure felt like a bribe but there was no ransom. He thought about going to the police, but if he did that their investigation might be detrimental to the school in question. He thought it was ironic that a letter to the Reporter was not included in the list of items. Why would the author not include her? Who had sent it? The serious question would be - who would benefit if the other state school went down? The answer was every team in the conference and every national powerhouse.

He was about to make a phone call he did not want to make. He was about to make a recommendation to a university president that was not going to be received well. This school's players were making the headlines in a negative way over the past year. Recent recruits had multiple arrest records. College award candidates were on video for disorderly conduct. Players who were drafted by NFL teams had only been mildly disciplined for their own sexual assaults. Transfer players with known assault backgrounds had been accepted by this same university.

The school president was his closest friend and strongest ally on the board and in executive committee. It would be the most difficult call he had ever had to make, but make it, he did. They talked for over an hour. At the end of the conversation, he recommended that the Other State University coach retire. It might be just enough to head-off an investigation that would ultimately involve the President himself.

The Commissioner told him that he could wait until all the recruits had signed. He told them they would survive because of the staff and their historical success. The sooner they acted the less danger for the President, who was now in shock. He too felt his stomach churn. He was afraid that what happened at the Baptist University would happen to his prized university. How exposed would he be? He wanted to know who sent the envelope. There had been no crime here, so looking for fingerprints was out of the questions. Besides, how many mail carriers had already touched the package?

The media would want to know why a coach with a high pre-season ranking in the prime of his career would want to retire. The Commissioner told the president to announce it for health reasons; the media would likely accept it. No media person wants to belittle someone who has cancer, or a heart condition. Who could ever fault someone wanting to spend time with his or her family? The Network would not want to see the Other State University under the spotlight; they had too great a fan base. He had heard that the NCAA was starting a commission against campus sexual assault and he would personally recommend someone from the Other State University to represent the conference. It would give them an "inside" person.

The thing that scared the Commissioner was that the person who sent the letter did not have to be a person of power. Could any person research any program for derogatory information? The internet and FOIA requests have allowed the common man access to information that could be used for damning purposes. He would need to announce at the next conference meeting how vulnerable the schools and the coaches truly were.

The Commissioner was bothered by the threat. The truth was that he was afraid he would get eight more packages like the one he received. He thought it might be from the Baptist University, but there were too many similarities between what the Baptist University had experienced and the proposed threats from "Ronald McDonald." Did the pseudonym have any secret meaning? He was planning on a long run when he got home.

Goal #2 would not be accomplished for a while.

The FCS AD

(July 2017, Two states away from Texas)

The President wanted to meet face to face in his office for their next meeting. The AD stuffed his stress ball in his back pocket. They were going to be a sounding board for one another as they discussed the possibility of this controversial hiring. The AD told the president that he appreciated the interest and help, but most importantly, his open mind.

The AD said, "To recap, something changed the Regents' plan between May to October regarding their Coach. I have ruled out the theory that some of the Regents acted on their own. Their board was full of C-level executives and business owners who would not tolerate rogue decision-making."

The President asked, "Do you think it was a threat of possible sanctions from the NCAA?" He leaned forward in his chair, resting his elbows on the edge of his desk.

"No," said the AD. "The NCAA does nothing quietly. They would go public; since they love to portray that they are on top of issues and investigations. Besides, they do not have any policies about sexual assaults nor, as a side note, any policies on random drug testing." He took the stress ball from his pocket and began squeezing it like a pumping heart.

The President was trying to be funny, "...and gun brandishing and exposure during massages."

The AD laughed but continued diplomatically, "I think the conference applied the pressure. Timeline and logic makes sense. Every major decision and action that the Regents had to make, occurred prior to or after conference meetings and events. Somebody or somebodies wanted the scandal over. They were not going to wait a year to see the coach come back and start the media circus all over. Publically, the Commissioner was using language from the conference by-laws. That was the clue. They wanted to see the Baptist University implement institutional control."

"What is the motivation to get rid of one person? Why not just vote out the whole administration?" The President's questions were getting more thorough and serious - he slowly rocked in his seat as he processed the events.

"The Baptist University President was terminated; its AD terminated, two staffers terminated and the story continued. Once the Regents were willing to sacrifice the Coach, the story changed course." The AD picked up steam and started to speak excitedly. "It was always a university problem, but the media turned it into a football problem because college football is what sells. The Regents caved because the conference forced their hands. They could not tolerate the pressure. They operated from fear of being kicked out of the conference. The conference needed more teams, not fewer. If the conference kicks the school out, they'd have to show cause. The Baptist school would tie the whole thing up in court. The conference would have to prove that sexual assaults were less prevalent at the other schools. The information that was provided in the conference school's security reports shows that could be a losing argument. At the end of the day when the dust settles, the conference would not kick the Baptist School out for sexual assaults because it needed the school to stay in the conference because at the time twelve teams were needed for a conference championship game. Instead, the blame needed to be placed somewhere else or on someone else. The problem is that they placed the blame for all of the sexual assaults on the Coach, who ultimately did nothing wrong when it came to sexual assaults by his players.   But he could only be blamed for "creating a culture" that encouraged the behavior of sexual assaults? ....hell does that mean? " He threw up his hands accidently sending the stress ball flying.

He paused and asked as he retrieved the stress ball, "Who benefits when a coach like that is terminated?"

"Every other school in the conference," replied the President. "They get the recruits. They get one more win. They get better televised games at better televised times. More wins means better bowl games, which in turn, means more revenue." He slapped his hands together.

"When the problem goes away, who benefits?" The AD asked already knowing the answer and what the President would say.

"The Commissioner. The focus goes away from the conference and so does the media attention. When the media attention goes away, the Commissioner can go back to his basic duties of representing, managing and planning."

Both men fell silent.

"Is there anything else to add?" asked the President.

"Do I need to add anything else?," queried the AD. "But he proceeded: My gut tells me that there was something personal, but we will never know. It really doesn't matter. The fact that they withheld six million dollars in revenue from the Baptist University tells me they were showing they had conference control and all of the power. If the Commissioner can pressure a couple Regents who can advise the whole board that everyone's problems will go away by sacrificing one football coach, then why not go that route? He becomes the scapegoat," the AD concluded. He took his index finger and made a slashing motion across his throat.

"I'm sitting here at ninety percent in favor. I just want to see the lawsuit concluded to get me over that last ten percent. What do you want to do?" the President asked.

There it was that funny feeling in his knee again. The AD leaned back in his chair, "I want to hire the coach."

The Coach
(August 2017, Central Texas)

He awoke to daylight and slowly looked at the alarm clock on his bedside table. He could hear the quiet breathing of his wife next to him. It had been almost a year and half since the Coach had had a decent night's sleep. Today, when he got out of bed, there would be spring in his step. He sat on the edge of the bed. It was a new day. He had been released from the lawsuit without prejudice. When his attorney conveyed the details of the release, the Coach's mind drifted in all of the legalese. The outcome meant only one thing to him: that his name was cleared and it was proof that he had no responsibility for the sexual misbehaviors of his players.

As he swung his legs out of bed, his foot hit something on the floor. It was his coaching cap from the Baptist University. He bent down to pick up. He sat and stared at it. He fought against the emotion and forced back the tears that filled his eyes. Finally, turning the hat in his hands, he said softly to himself, "I'm going to miss you Baptist Nation. Happy Trails." He shoved the cap way under his bed. A new chapter was beginning.

His agent had been working to find football coaching opportunities for him. He had been offered a coaching job with a professional football team in Canada. Not exactly a dream job, but it was a start and he was excited about the opportunity.   He could not remember the last time he had to wear long underwear. But he didn't care how cold it would be; he could not wait to be on the sideline again. His agent was working out all the details. He knew it was going to be colder and the field and the rules would be slightly different. But it was football. And he loved coaching football.

The Reporter
(August 2017, New England)

In her office, she was making her schedule for the next couple months. Her book was released. She was deciding in which cities she would hold book signings. The book was a bucket list item she could check off now: two years in the making. It was the most time she had ever spent on a story. The book had been easy. She had had all the articles, and all the contact information from all the victims because of the police reports. The book, however, was able to provide more detail of the events that transpired at Baptist University than any one of her articles or on-air broadcasts.

The "no comments," or vague information from the Baptist University and from the police departments were frustrating to her. While she had prepared herself for those responses, they did create minor obstacles that she would have to navigate. Because she was so good at her profession, she would be able to "connect the dots" of the unsaid conversations and deliver *her* storyline for her readers.

The Reporter was amused by the Regents' involvement. She thought they were trying to kiss up to her. When they had their comments and reactions available to her, she questioned their motivation. Were they trying to get her to like them? Were they trying to convince her that the Regents had no responsibility for what had transpired at their university? Were they hoping she would not write anything derogatory about them? She is a reporter, it is her job to investigate and report. She smiled because she knew she was more than just a reporter; she was a creative journalist who could take events and masterfully create a storyline.

The Regents were helpful in giving her information about the drug usage and lack of drug testing. Even though the testing is not required by the NCAA, the Regents were quick to point out how stringent the university was on drug usage. Using drugs was a violation of the school's student conduct policy. She found it humorous, if not hypocritical, that this was the same student conduct policy that informed students that underage drinking and sexual activity should be subject to biblical principles; the same student policy that the government's Office of Civil Rights made them discard so sexual assault victims would have amnesty if they were found drinking or smoking marijuana while having premarital sex.

"What a cluster" the Reporter thought. Football players, who are governed by NCAA rules, should be disciplined by a University for violating the student conduct for using drugs, but girls who used the same drugs were given amnesty from the student conduct policy by the federal government. The Reporter didn't care. The general public would never accept the notion that a former Texas high school football coach could turn around an irrelevant college football program with hard work, making practice and games fun, creating a high scoring offense, getting the most out of his players and recruiting players who had a competitive edge. No, the general public, the people who watched the Network, wanted it to be something else. The public wanted to believe that somehow the Coach was cheating. That somehow the Coach was taking short-cuts. The Reporter's mission had been to expose how the university had failed to protect women, and how the Coach had created a culture in which the football players could get away with it. She had accomplished her mission.

As she thumbed thru her own book, she told God, "I have my own book now too. I wrote mine personally."

The Writer
(August 2017, Capitol City, Texas)

A few months had passed since the Writer had called the Software Developer from her home to see what was developing with the hopes of another story. She was shooting for a "happy hour" roof top meeting to be scheduled. The Software Developer had told her he would be sending FOIA requests on her behalf using her name and address. The information received from the requests was supposed to be sent directly to her because her name and address were used.   At least that was what the Software Developer had told her.

The early retirement announcement of the Other State School's coach paralleled when the Software Developer had first laid out the plans. When the Writer did her own preliminary research, she was shocked about how accurately the Software Developer's information was. The coach from the Other State University had a track record of recruiting players with questionable character. He too had had players arrested on sexual assault and physical assault charges. The actions were eerily similar to those for which the Baptist University was accused. The coach from Other State University actually brought players back after they served offseason suspensions. The Writer was unaware that the Software Developer had also sent the package to the Commissioner. She had been made unaware because the Booster ordered the Software Developer not to tell her.

Her call went into voicemail. Fifteen minutes later, however, the Software Developer returned her call. The Writer was disappointed with the update she received. He gave her a quick rundown of what had transpired.

The Booster had told the Software Developer to stand down with any heavy pressure or follow-up; the Booster said to hold off in actually sending the requests until the situation took its natural course. The goal was to remove the coach; not to destroy the program and make *it* irrelevant. The Other State University coach had retired quietly - no questions asked. And no one was going interrogate someone with health issues. The conference still needed two powerhouses. The Booster determined that it was time for the State University to start winning again. Little tweaks were all that was needed to change the balance of power. If those little tweaks did not accomplish the goal, the Booster could always take more drastic measures

The Writer and the Software Developer agreed to stay in touch. They would let each other know if the story started to gain traction. The Software Developer told her that a possible sexual assault case could be developing and an indictment may follow. The "Other State" had grand juries as well; however, the prosecuting attorneys were unwilling to be as assertive and aggressive as the ones in Central Texas. So he was unsure if the case would really be brought to light. The Software Developer had no idea if what he told the Writer was true. He was just getting paid by the Booster to follow instructions and mentioning the "possible case" was simply part of his instructions.

FCS AD

(Late August 2017, Two states away from Texas)

Because of vacations and the start of school, the FCS AD and the President had not been able to meet for several weeks. The President was unavailable when the AD texted him the news that the Coach had been released from the lawsuit. His name was cleared. The FCS University could now offer the Coach a position. But they needed to sit down and go through the terms of the contract and how they were going to deal with the onslaught of media people who would, no doubt, come to their campus questioning the hire. The AD loved the challenge and the fight. He did not care and had nothing to lose; he was fearless. His main concern, however, was how would he avoid cursing like a drunken sailor if the media started to make him angry.

The President texted back and told the AD to be in his office in an hour. Both men cleared their schedules. The AD was so well prepared for the meeting with the President that their meeting lasted only two hours. They finished agreeing what they could offer, and how the process would play out. They had the plan in place when a tweet hit the AD's phone announcing the Coach was taking a job in Canada. The Canadian Professional team made an announcement welcoming their new coach and that they looked forward to an explosive display of offensive football.

"Hell fire and save the matches!" the AD shouted. He jumped out of his chair so fast that he felt a dull pain back in his knee. Both men were so disappointed. The President was upset that he had spent the time in vain. The AD was bummed that a golden opportunity was now thrown out the window. He had finished the contract with a great offer. He was even rehearsing his announcement speech. Both men shook hands. The disheartened look on both their faces told the story. The AD returned to his office with a slight, painful limp.

The AD was devastated. He had no idea their window of opportunity was so small. He held the file on the Coach in his hands. He was headed to the shredder at the other end of the hall. His phone rang distracting him as he started a new conversation with another member of his department. He headed out to the parking lot towards his car. He was still engaged in deep conversation. He threw the folder on the passenger seat, started the car and said good-bye to the person on the other end of the line. He realized he had forgotten to shred the folder, but walking back would only aggravate his knee. He would deal with it tomorrow.

Later that night when he was eating dinner with his family, his phone vibrated. Strangely his knee felt better. It was a text from the President. He closed his eyes and said a short prayer. His family reminded him that they had already blessed the food. He had a smile a mile wide. The text read, "Call me. Canada deal fell through."

The Advocate

(Late August 2017, Pacific Northwest)

All her hard work had paid off. The petitions, speaking engagements, and the daily activity on social media awarded her a position on the NCAA Commission to combat campus sexual assaults. It was truly an honor. She would do her very best to help keep violent athletes out of the college sports. She was grateful and looked forward to serving in the position.

When the Coach was hired by a professional football team in Canada, the Advocate had been furious. She lashed out against the hiring. It did not matter to her that the position was professional or even in a different country; she claimed the Coach might influence and threaten the minds of grown men to be more violent. She stated that he would warp the minds of his new coaching staff.

She personally had not seen a change in the Coach's beliefs or attitude. She blogged, if the Coach turned around a losing Canadian Professional team, the temptation would be too great for a college football team to want to hire the Coach.

She charged that the Coach should never be allowed to coach again. Any organization that hired him was risking the safety of women in the interest of winning games.

There was no official commission to combat the Coach. She would chair the committee if one actually existed. It was clear that she had made a personal goal to try to prevent the Coach from ever being hired. Every conference was represented on the NCAA Commission. She had access to speak her voice and use her influence to any other committee member.

She thought she had reconciled her personal situation but reconciliation requires forgiveness. She was adamantly opposed to everything the Coach did or anything that included him. She had never even met the Coach. She never talked or interviewed any of his former players about him. The amount of energy required to maintain that high a level of opposition had to be fueled by a power source: hers was hatred. And if hatred is present, it means there never was forgiveness. She had projected her hatred onto the Coach.

The Coach

(Today, Central Texas)

It had been a roller coaster of emotions for the Coach. He was so close to his next big thing and so close to the horrendous nightmare being over. When his cell phone rang, the Coach did not recognize the number. He barely recognized the area code. He answered the phone anyway. It was probably the media. Even though the media calls had died down months ago, the Coach had learned to prepare himself so that he would not be caught off guard.

The AD introduced himself and his title at the FSC University. The AD was normally cool and collected, so he was surprised at the anxiety he felt when he made the call. The AD asked, "Coach, do you know where FCS University is?" He was embarrassed that the question might be insulting to the Coach. The Coach's emotions had been in full swing, but the Coach still found the question humorous.

"Yes sir, I sure do," as he chuckled. It's still in the United States last time I checked." His quick wit was never too far away, even in the face of the setback

Instantly the mood lightened. The AD got right to the point. He said, "Coach, I want to hire you to be our head football coach. You know we are not a Power 5 conference team, but we pay a competitive salary for an FCS school and the contract will be heavy in incentives. It would be a three year contract with the school having an option in years in four and five. It is still Division I and we are not that far from Texas."

The Coach paused. He had been emotionally down this path before. He had a bunch of questions. His biggest concern was how the FCS school would deal with the media. The Coach was not sure how to phrase his question because surely the school would have thought about media onslaught. He asked, "Do you have a plan for dealing with the negative attention you are about to get from the media?" The Coach was again feeling the burden of having to deal with a situation where he couldn't defend himself.

The AD replied, "Coach, we believe you did nothing wrong in the area of sexual assault. We have done our internal investigation. We've answered all of our questions. We are ready to stand behind our hiring decision regardless of the pressure. We have all of our Title IX processes in place. We have processes in place for the other off-the-field issues. It's simple. We are ready. The right thing to do is to have you coach again, and do so at our school".

There it was again. He heard his mother's words of instruction coming back. It felt right. The Coach knew all the details would be worked out by his agent and the school's attorneys. Tonight was about making the decision. He was quiet for a few seconds before he said, "I'm ready. Let's go win us some football games."

The FCS AD

(Sometime in the near future, Two states away from Texas)

The school was too small to have a media press room. They used a smaller lecture hall instead. The AD stood behind the podium wearing his best suit. He stood straight. His knee felt great. The "press" room was about three quarters full. He knew the negative criticism would be coming from the national media. Since his conference was not a Power 5 School and did not have a contract with the Network, he expected only few members of the national media to be present for the announcement. He was wrong; there were more national reporters than he predicted. He didn't care. He had hired the man he wanted.

He welcomed the crowd. He thanked them for being there. Then he said:

"Ladies and Gentlemen –

Today I bring great news by announcing Coach as the new head coach for our FCS team. I want to address what everyone in the room is thinking. We have done a thorough investigation of the Coach's tenure at Baptist University. We have been unable to find any situation where the Coach ever had direct contact with a victim, where he ever discouraged someone from reporting the information or going to the police. In fact, we have discovered just the opposite. The Coach is on record for encouraging victims to press charges with the authorities. We have also found no situation where the Coach ever played an athlete once the player was found responsible for committing a sexual assault. These are the same conclusions reached by the Baptist University, and we can prove it."

The Coach has been trained in *our* Title IX processes and he can keep them and follow their requirements. We have discussed in detail the processes for other off-the-field issues and the Coach can commit to following those practices. He will oversee his coaching staff when they are hired and he will make sure they will follow the policies as well.

It is my position that no person can purposely control another human being without physically constraining them, which by the way is against the law. The Coach is responsible for what the players do on the field. He cannot control how they conduct their lives when they are home or in their dorms or apartments. It is my position that the culture by which a player can be influenced involves his parents, his siblings, the neighborhood he grew up in, how he was raised, the movies he watches, the songs he listens to, the friends he keeps. It involves what the player does in his free time and the choices he makes. To say that a coach at this point in a young student athlete's life has more influence than any of the aforementioned – is preposterous. A coach can be responsible for a winning culture or a losing culture. He has the potential to be a father figure to some of the players individually, but only if time allows. *We* are pleased to begin a new era in FCS University football.

You all are going to have lots of questions. The Coach is still contractually bound about what he can say. If you want to ask any questions, the Coach will be available for one-on-one interviews. You must submit your questions in advance. The list of acceptable questions and interview times can be coordinated through my office. Please call my administrative assistant. If you ask a question that was not on your reviewed submittal of questions, your interview will end immediately and you will be asked to leave."

Our energies and time are focused on our tomorrows - not our yesterdays. We wish the Coach much success and look forward to him being here"

Thank you. And go Mascots!"

The Coach
(Sometime in the near future, Rural City, Texas)

The Coach pulled his car down a street that had been in need of maintenance for at least twenty-five years. Each small home vaguely resembled the other. Every fourth or fifth home had become a vacant lot. Original homes were either knocked down or burned in a fire. Some of the homes were boarded up with plywood. It was a rough area, but the Coach had seen plenty of these areas over the last twenty years.

He was invited into one of the houses at the end of the street. When he stepped inside, he was immediately in the living room, which was small, though still large enough to have a recliner and a couch that faced a flat screen television mounted on the wall. It was the home of a recruit.

The recruit's mother sat in the recliner. She had offered the coach a glass of water, but he always replied "maybe later." The recruit sat on the couch. His younger brother and younger sister sat on the couch next to him. They were wide-eyed and had a lot of nervous energy. They had never had an older white man in their living room before, so this was a new experience. An older brother sat in a fold-out metal chair. He was shirtless and wore pajama bottoms.

The Scapegoat

The Coach started the conversation with small talk but he liked to cut to get down to the heart of the issues in real discussions. He said, "Son, I know a lot of schools, good football teams, want you to play for them. Most of them want you to play defensive back. Am I correct?"

"Yes, sir," said the recruit.

"Most of them have probably said that at six feet, you don't have the height to play quarterback but since you are a two-way starter and a heckuva defensive back they want to see you at safety. Is that correct?"

"Yes, sir," said the recruit nodded in agreement.

"The truth is son, you can flat out play. You make great reads. You can throw on the run. You know when to step up in the pocket and when to scramble." He thought he heard the older brother mutter "mmmmm hmmm," but the coach wasn't sure.

"You know, Coach, I have some really big FBS schools looking at me. Mainly defense, but they have said if I grow another inch or more before I enroll, they may give me a chance at QB. I also want to be close enough for my family to watch me play," the recruit said. "I like the idea of playing on television."

The Coach said, "Me too. The reality is- you need to look at their recruiting classes. Not just this year but the year before. If they already have a quarterback each year and one slotted in this upcoming class, they are just feeding you a line of bull."

The older brother cleared his throat, but the recruit shot him a stare that said, "Shut up and keep quiet."

"Truth," the recruit said. "I know I can play QB, but what makes you so sure when others won't give me a fair chance without conditions?"

The Coach said, "Because you remind of a kid I had ten years ago. He had the same skill sets as you. He loved the game. He played "all-in." He went on to win the Heisman."

The recruit did not say anything; he was visualizing what it would be like when he won a college football game.

The Coach continued saying, "Son I like to have fun. I like to have fun at practice. I like everything to go at top speed. Game speed. I like to score. I like to light up the scoreboard. I play fast. I like players who like to play with an edge. I like quarterbacks who like to run and who like to throw. But most of all, I like to win. Winning is fun."

The recruit's mama was quietly nodding in agreement. The recruit leaned forward. He put his head in his hands for a couple seconds. He leaned back in the couch. He looked up at the ceiling. He then leaned forward looked the Coach in the eye and said, "Ok. Coach, I want to play for you."

The Coach shook his hand. He gave a quick wink. He responded, "All right then. Let's go get you some fast receivers who will catch your passes. I know right where to start... ."

Afterward

(745-750 BC, Israel Desert)

The boy had been warned by his mother not to wonder too far from the tents when he would get up and play in the mornings. He was a member of a clan of nomads. His mother was concerned about the threat of wild animals. On this particular morning he was feeling extra brave as he walked to some desert foothills until he could barely see the group of tents where the rest of the clan members were still sleeping.

Engrossed in his imagination, the boy began to play. The wind changed and the boy thought he heard the sound of soft crying. He searched the landscape for the source of the sound; seeing nothing, he continued to play. He heard the sound again, it was a bleat. It was definitely a bleat from a goat. He knew the sound well. He squinted his eyes hoping to see further in the distance when his eyes focused on a small bush.

He approached the bush, cautiously at first, and then he ran as fast as he could. When he got to the bush, he saw the goat. He bent down and petted the goat. The goat's wool was dirty. It was matted from years of desert dust. The goat clearly had been attacked and injured. Dried blood had hardened under his neck and throat. The boy could tell it was malnourished and the goat wobbled when the boy tried to have the goat stand on all four legs. The boy held out the palm of his hand. The goat licked the palm.

Overwhelmed with joy, the boy picked up the goat and put him over his shoulders and ran. He ran as fast as his legs would go. Shouting loudly as he approached the camp, he yelled, "Mama! Mama! I have found a goat. Mama, he is good one!"

Epilogue
(Present Day, United States)

Network Executive – In the aftermath of firing ten percent of its on air-staff, subscriptions continue to decline as viewers continue to prefer online programming. The Network purchased a heavy interest in Technology Company that specializes in streaming video. The Network Executive oversees that division.

The Reporter - She has shifted her attention and her media focus to the ten universities she had targeted in 2015. She is still pursuing law suits against certain schools in Michigan and Indiana.

The Commissioner – After receiving a contract extension from the conference, the Commissioner is satisfied that conference has a championship football game even though it still does not have twelve teams. He is monitoring the FBI investigations for college basketball to see how the conference will be affected.

The State University, Blogger-Radio Host, Booster and Software Developer - They are enjoying their rise to the top half of the conference with a winning record. They are patiently waiting to upheave the Other State University.

The Writer – She monitors the internet and still tracks college sexual assaults daily basis. The accusations against the NFL broadcasters are an interest to her. She has a new book coming out soon.

The Advocate – She continues to speak at schools and athletic programs. Several of the coaches have been fired at the schools where she spoke, so she is careful not to "call out" specific coaches anymore as she serves on the committee to combat sexual violence.

The Regents - They, along with the administration, continue to navigate thru the remaining lawsuits and Department of Education compliance investigations. They are patient with their stellar hires in a new President and Head Football Coach and the Title IX progress their school made.

Author Comments

This was an incredibly difficult book to write because college sexual assaults have been politicized and there is more rhetoric and talk about the issue, than there is action of trying to decrease the number of incidents. Seventy-eight percent of all college sexual assaults involve alcohol and drugs. Seventy-three percent of all college sexual assaults involve freshman and sophomores. Nineteen percent of all sexual assaults are perpetrated by male student athletes but they only comprise four percent of the student population.

These numbers are alarming. You have to be twenty-one to buy alcohol, and eighteen to purchase cigarettes in most states. Each state ranges from sixteen-eighteen years old as the determining age for sex with a minor. There are so many proponents that want to eliminate campus sexual assaults but I have never heard a single one argue to rise the age minor age to twenty-one. I want to know why? Who or what is causing their fear to take such a radical stance?

This author is a proponent of Title IX investigations and the threat of chemical castration. But it is sickening that we no longer hold those to blame, personally responsible. So I hope that I step on everyone's toes. My belief is that everybody is to blame.

Male college students and male student athletes: If your college experience is based on the number of women you have sex with during your time at college, shame on you for your worthless standards. If you think of women only as objects to be used for your lustful pleasure, shame on you. If you think you can have casual sex with anyone without it having an emotional impact on you or the woman, shame on you for being shallow. If you think your only ability to "score" with a female student is to get them intoxicated, shame on you for being selfish. If you watch porn on a regular basis and think that most women have the same sex drive that you do, shame on you for believing the lie.

Female college students: If you think "sexting naked pictures of yourself or offering sexual favors to guys as ways to get them to like you, you are putting your female sisters at risk, because the guys will think all women behave like you - Shame on you for your carelessness. If you are willing to engage in "talking" or having sex with a guy without even dating him, shame on you for cheapening sex and putting other girls at risk by sending the guys the message that sex is cheap and easy. If you abuse Title IX provisions and accuse a male student for assault when the sex was really regret by you, shame on you for trying to ruin the life of another person.

Administration: If your attitude toward a Title IX incident is just to make the problem go away as quickly as possible, shame on you for your lack of sympathy and compassion. If your Title IX caseload is so cumbersome that issues can't be addressed in a timely fashion, shame on you for not allocating more resources. If your only care is getting a student transferred or off your campus, shame on you for having such a selfish attitude and unwillingness to solve a bigger problem

Coaches: If you enable your players and don't set expectations for rules to be followed, shame on you for belittling them by being their friend instead of being their leader. If you encourage cheating to justify winning, shame on you for devaluing them as people and treating them as objects. If you encourage your players to entertain recruits by getting them drunk and laid, shame on you for your immoral standards.

Office of Civil Rights: If you think Title IX cases can be resolved in sixty days when criminal cases can take over a year, shame on you for your naivety. If your guidance is only to point out what a school is doing wrong and not offering standards to achieve, shame on you for your unwillingness to truly help. If you think a Title IX coordinator or adjudicator can successfully conduct a fair investigation without running into Family Education Rights and Privacy Act (FERPA) legal constraints, shame on you for not giving them ample legal tools to perform their jobs. Shame on you for being so quick to judge and penalize but so slow to truly help and be proactive. If you really want to help, make all the schools publically report the number of Title IX investigations and the number of each verdicts (favoring the accused, victim and dismissed)resulting from the cases.

College Football Fans everywhere – While college football is the greatest game ever played, if our Saturday is ruined when our team loses, and if we wish for other players on opposing teams to get hurt or arrested or flunk, shame on us for making this game an idol. It is only a game.

Fathers of sons – It is time for the double standard on how we raise sons and daughters to stop. The promiscuity of your son should have the same expectation level as your daughter. Quit applauding him for his sexual activity. The first step in training is to model the behavior yourself. Make sure he understands what "respect" means. Every male says that he respects women. Talk is cheap; it needs to be exemplified in his behavior. How he wants people to treat his mother and sister is how he needs to treat the women he dates. Tonight some other guy is seeing your son's future girlfriend/wife, how that woman is considered is going to affect the relationship she has with your son. Teach your son the same responsibility of caring for the women he dates.

Fathers of daughters – I am not going to blast you, but I'm going to beg you – love your little girls. Remind them how beautiful they are. Kiss their foreheads constantly. Instill confidence in their characters. Go deep into your conversations with them so that your daughter will know she can talk to you about anything, including mistakes, and when she has been wronged. Be there for her and tell her you love her again and again. Protect her by preparing her for dangerous situations. Before she leaves for college, remind her that boys are liars and to be cautious about college partying. Guys like it when girls drink because they know it loosens inhibitions. Be her father first, then her friend. Be her hero. Because if there is anything worth fighting for in life – it is her!

Final Words - If we are going to take the position that female students are unable to give consent if they have been drinking, and females have the right to rescind their consent at any time, we are forced to acknowledge that thousands of sexual assaults occur on our campuses every weekend. The problem will never be addressed.

At the end of the day, we all need to encourage women who are victims to 1) get rape exams and 2) report the incidents to the police. Yes, reporting to the police is difficult. Yes, having to tell parents is even more difficult. And having to relive tragic events is the most difficult, but it is the best path we have to drive the number of sexual assaults down. Look at what has happened in Hollywood and in broadcasting. Pressing charges by coming forward creates change!

Made in the USA
Columbia, SC
12 January 2018